# SUNSET VILLAGE

FRANK SARGESON

# Sunset Village

AUCKLAND UNIVERSITY PRESS
OXFORD UNIVERSITY PRESS

First published in 1976
by Martin Brian & O'Keeffe Ltd
37 Museum Street London WC1

© Frank Sargeson 1976

ISBN 0 589 00962 1

Printed in Great Britain by
Bristol Typesetting Co Ltd Bristol

# CONTENTS

# I

Despite a readiness to agree about the settlement's many disadvantages, it was never Mrs Trigger's habit to complain about the flat which had been allocated her. And how else could it be? —that was to say, if it was conceded that she was a person in need of pensioner housing. For although the slope of the site was toward the cold south, it was Mrs Trigger's good fortune to be highest of all, almost perched you might say—where from her wide window she could observe every unit; or almost. A knitting person, it was her great kindness to knit for anybody who could afford to buy the wool. For women she knitted cardigans, frocks, belts, slippers, bedsocks, mittens, tea-cosies: for men, bedsocks only: she never charged for her work: and it should go without saying that it was her habit to knit while she sat comfortably at what her deceased husband would have called her o.p.; that is to say, observation post. Infantry-sergeant Trigger, a tall heavyweight and very florid, he had been vain about a fine head of black hair that waved, and also shone like polished ebony: in the army he had always been absurdly called Hair Trigger. By his wife he had never been called other than just ' Trigger '!

Across a jazz pattern of roofs and gardens there was a long view of farmlands that were often green and always rolling—and rolled indeed until halted by a moderate mountain range which when the weather permitted was seen as a mild blue. A view that was often very lovely; and there were times when Mrs Trigger paid lip-tribute. But the great natural world as one supposed it would be seen by the astronauts was a spectacle on which she seldom focused. She preferred what was much closer to hand. It has been said of great novelists that it is part of their power to see through brick walls; and neither was Mrs Trigger deterred, nor by tiled roofs. You might reflect that the

7

flats were all uniform, and the difference in furnishings was of no great consequence; and so it would be as well if extravagant notions about Mrs Trigger's gift of X-ray eyes were dispensed with. But that didn't help much: because without ever entering any flat except her own ('no dear, you come and see *me*'— and wasn't the climb-up which a visit entailed only her due?), what Mrs Trigger consistently saw was what went on: the *mise-en-scène* could be taken for granted.

It was for all that not much to be doubted that the secret of Mrs Trigger's 'knowing' so much was to be discovered more in lively natural gifts enriched by a lifetime's experience of human behaviour: possession of superhuman powers could be written off. Appearances suggested somebody very formidable, a no-nonsense kind of widowed female of a certain age with a square jaw, grim features and a vast robust bosom. But what was on view was not wholly to be depended upon, and it was a part of the lady's quality distinction or what have you to be herself keenly aware that she was *never* to be compared with what she sometimes defined in her thoughts (and very occasionally in her speech), as the average human vegetable. It had been her lifetime's discretion to conceal from friends and acquaintances that she had been sole sister among ten brothers: after five boys (colts, as their father who bred horses called them), had come Amy, a filly: afterwards, five more colts. It had required remarkably few years for Miss Amy, a precocious child, to become capable of the reflection that things were not quite as people supposed: the public total of colts was one short: and such was her self-perception that before she had finished with being a schoolgirl it was her wit to mutter to herself, 'Well, a miss is as good as a mile.' Strangers were at times confused by absent-minded information that there were eleven in the family, all boys. But for all that compensations were many, often sweet and sometimes absurd. After all, ten husky he-man brothers (although it was afterwards to turn out, as will presently be seen, there was an exception to this general rule), and one dear sister! Birthday presents could be lavish and expensive (and sometimes in her secret thoughts superfluous feminine rubbish)! She dissembled and acquired the habit; and by the time she had become a probationer nurse all had been thoroughly worked out, placed under proper control. Once she

8

had temporarily lost her head and heart: another probationer, a pretty little prattling blonde, a powder-puff if ever there was one, who had fainted when required to remove and empty a bedpan: without her friend Amy's passionate support she would have become a sad loss to nursing.

But never mind all that now. As Mrs Trigger she had survived. Dissembling had become a habit, a second nature which suited her. Why, bless him, Trigger had never in their married lifetime suspected a thing; and for her part she had never quite recovered from her surprise that after a surplus of brothers she could tolerate the sight and sound of a man about the house (and let alone his presence in her bed). But there had been foresight in her choice of a partner—after all armies are for fighting, regular soldiers must reckon on long interruptions to regular leave. And yet, men around, indeed one man, a husband, could be handy and comforting. As for bed, that was also two-way: a nuisance sometimes perhaps, but flattering—like her brothers' birthday attentions. It had been her habit to help very little, and clumsy Trigger, broad-beamed and corpulent, needed help. He did his best, pleased at all times when at last he was comforted: and perhaps in his dim way he perceived that he had for the most part comforted himself: as for the wife, it never occurred to him to inquire whether *she* had been comforted—although subtly she more or less always was: she never found herself with anything much to complain about (that was to say provided Trigger had not forgotten to keep his bedsocks on, for he suffered from nasty cold feet). Sometimes thoughts of a child would enter her mind, but not often; there were never any signs. Also it was seldom when Trigger was at his endeavours that she did not remember and think tenderly of the little baby blonde, the pretty little lollypop.

It was probably on account of her background that she would sometimes think she had been widowed by Trigger's having died in the saddle.

From the standard tenancy agreement which all were obliged to sign, it could be inferred that by the municipal authority it was taken for granted that pensioners had arrived at a time of life when ' all that sort of thing ' would or should be over and done with. Tenants, married or single, were prohibited from affording accommodation, no matter how fleeting, to other persons of either sex unless there was a formal permission from the municipal landlord. But perhaps it could be supposed that the implied interdiction upon immorality did not figure quite so ominously in the municipal mind, and what the rule amounted to was that you were being told to desist from any irregular relationship which had been your comfort in the past, perhaps a warmth with implied under- and over-tones of generosity kindness affection sympathy—which might well have been one good reason why in old age you preferred to remain alive, when a long long solacing sleep without dreams might well have been a more attractive proposition.

It should however be noticed that among tenants this rule was not much mentioned, and only very occasionally railed against: and much more a topic for conversation was the prohibition against the keeping of pets of any description. It can perhaps go without saying that the keeping of hens for eggs was also totally interdicted. But harder to understand was a ban upon the planting of shrubs in the great green spaces of lawn; also upon the transformation of any strip of green outside your door in to a herbaceous border—although this last was not strictly enforced provided the Council was informed about the number and kind of ornamental or vegetable plants you intended to grow. And perhaps one good reason for no great concern about the prohibition against staying visitors was a feeling that the least said the better—that it could be anybody's problem to know for certain whether the rule was being disregarded or not. After all if your visitor arrived quietly enough late at night and left before daybreak who was likely to know? Or there might be a leave-taking quite *late* in the morning—and who was to say that he or she as might be the case hadn't arrived when you were busy eating your breakfast and had failed to notice? And this last might have indeed been a watertight strategy if it hadn't been for the sharp observing eyes of Mrs Trigger.

But not that the lady was the only tenant whose habit it was to observe keenly as a preliminary to much thought about many interesting variations in human behaviour—although without much doubt nobody could be reckoned a serious competitor apart from Brixton: Brixton Brake, sallow and sharp-featured, thin as a

greyhound, and showing a good deal of light and lithe greyhound
movement: he wore saddle-tweed trousers and a soft-leather
jacket, and all topped off by a close-fitting cap with a long shading
peak. Nobody (it was said) had ever seen him without his cap,
and there were many speculations about what kind of hair underneath, or whether perhaps he had none: or he might perhaps be
covering up some unpleasant deformity, even perhaps some
nasty non-healing sore. His smooth youthful features were by
some also put down against him—was he, could he possibly be,
of an age to make him eligible for pensioner housing? But perhaps
at the heart of Brixton's mystery were the binoculars which were
always slung about his neck. He had never been seen to raise
them to his eyes, just as nobody meeting him about the streets had
ever seen him without them. It had even been said that motorists,
miles out in the country, had seen him on the top of some hill,
standing like a statue while he looked into the far distance—
but never with the aid of his binoculars. And perhaps what it
all added up to was a strange kind of hint that if circumstances
had been right he might well have figured as a modern urban
guerilla general on active service.

But according to the villagers he was for the most part just
'creepy.' Nor did the shoes he wore help matters, for they were
soft-leather with a sheen like silk and the thinnest of soft-rubber
soles: they looked more like indoor slippers in which nobody
who appreciated the niceties of behaviour would be likely to
venture along the street. And perhaps the word venture is right,
because for Brixton, despite his years, life remained very much
a venture: official old age was a statistic of very little account.

But for the time being never mind about Brixton's appetite
and aptitude for ventures. Let it be emphasized instead there
was that about him which suggested a kind of male counterpart
to Mrs Trigger. And indeed, provided the weather was right,
the pair spent a good deal of their time in conversation—but
always depending upon the weather because never had Brixton
entered Mrs Trigger's premises, his visits being limited to an
approach to her while she knitted: he would relax outside her
window, with his elbow hooked over the sill. In full public view
there could never be any doubt about ready verbal exchanges
which would last sometimes for an hour and even longer.

Although nobody could be sure what their subjects were when all talk would cease upon the approach of another person. Often too for the villagers it was additional frustration that the pair were seen and heard to laugh—and surely apart from all else wasn't it bad manners for anyone who knew a good joke not to share it with his neighbours? And it is to be feared that much of the truth of the matter was that Mrs Trigger and Brixton were to a degree exhibitionist characters—you could almost say theatrical types who enjoyed putting on a show which villagers were free to enjoy or not just as they pleased: although always provided they kept their decent distance while the show lasted.

But for all that the villagers were wrong in their belief that it was the bad habit of this pair openly (even though out of ear-shot), to discuss the private affairs of other people: that is to say their neighbours in the settlement. It was in fact their practice never to name another person: individual persons were almost never discussed, and in any case would figure as ' he ' or ' she ': but it was much more usual for other people to be ' they '. Thus it was Brixton (who would prefix much of what he had to say with the statement, ' I don't know '—and then immediately contradict himself by demonstrating that he knew remarkably well indeed), who had said, ' If you ask me to put a name to it Mrs Trigger, I would say they're the affluent poor.'

Now to the reader it will be evident from this remark that Brixton was a good distance off from being another sample of the average human vegetable which often tended to figure in the thoughts of Mrs Trigger. Nor as a rule, having made a statement which compared very favourably with much that constantly assaults the citizen from so many varieties of media (and not excluding many spokesmen for ancestral institutions—political leaders parsons and priests parents schoolteachers presidents chairmen of this and that), was Brixton content to leave his apophthegm to take care of itself just as it had been uttered. Underlining was called for, and he was to be depended upon.

He didn't know, but he nonetheless went on to say, ' Where is the thing that opens and shuts they haven't got? Count up on your fingers beginning with the telly—and my God when I think what my old mum would have said!'

But on this question Mrs Trigger had no doubts, and was so

ready with her reply she overlooked her habit of confirming words of native wisdom with a reference to the deceased sergeant. 'The old lady would have thanked her lucky stars for benefits and godsends, Mr Brake, you mark my words.' And then, quickly remembering, she added, 'And I'll guarantee my Trigger would never have said a word different.'

At this stage of a difference Brixton would usually resign; but perhaps this day was itself different.

'Look Mrs Trig, it's life made easy and no need for six easy lessons—just a flick of the switch and you light up cook wash, all the box of tricks. And you know what I mean to include with that word box don't you Mrs Trig? They have it all handed on a plate. Now what if hens were allowed? Wouldn't *that* be a godsend? Feeding times, collecting the eggs. Pets to keep an eye on and make friends with and keep their minds off . . . Well I don't know Mrs Trig, but I mean left without having a cent left over to spend.'

Mrs Trigger waited until she had finished bothering over some stitches. 'I still say godsend, Mr Brake. And guess what you have forgotten to mention—which they could do without less comfortably than what you say. Where there's life there's hope—and I mean a Ticket, fifty cents invested each week, that costs two dollars each payday, and too much to afford. But never venture, Mr Brake, never venture . . .'

And it was as though her look confirmed what was often in his mind—that without mutual recognition their relationship could never have been so easy-going. Never venture! Well, he knew what it was to venture. None better! Where there was understanding you knew how you stood . . .

And yet perhaps after all there was never any clear rule about knowing how you stood. Brixton occupied an end flat in a row of three: at the other end there was Clementine, and in between Murray, Murray Piper—the MP as he was called: and although it might be said he more or less looked the part one could readily think, 'Yes, but not on the side of Labour, the *other* side.' A much shorter man than Brixton, Murray was a conservative-executive type, Chamber of Commerce, Rotary, all that sort of thing, a man who pulled his shirt cuffs down. And quite unlike Brixton, there was nothing to suggest that if he hadn't been his age he could have competed very successfully with any young man-woman in unisex clothing. Murray's outdoor suits were dated, seen to be a little seedy and frayed if you had the chance of close inspection; yet they would appear so freshly brushed and ironed you could have declared them only that day returned from the dry cleaner: also he wore shirts of many pastel colours. And out of all this encasing cloth and haberdashery Murray's face and head of soft sunset-red hair rose on the short thick stem of his neck like a great flower—something of exotic breed because his round face bloomed scarlet and was besides spotted with freckles. Always he smiled. And it was his smile which had been Brixton's undoing. For Brixton had supposed the smile was for him. But not at all, for everybody (and in this instance that also meant, for nobody). Murray's smile was a protection; and deceived as well by his eyes which were prominent and staring, Brixton (whose own eyes were hooded and retiring), hadn't understood. That smile said, keep off!—*not*, come on! And yet how could Murray with his hot red face be said to freeze people off? There was a time when Brixton had been asked inside; and more than that, invited to eat. And it was that evening, when he had been allowed to wash up while Murray dried that everything had come unstuck. For Brixton, busy with his chore, had turned in Murray's direction and found him not with the tea-towel as expected—no, instead a length of cord which he held at each end; and while the world buzzed in Brixton's ears Murray had pushed his smiling face a little closer, lifting the cord a little higher as he said, ' I could kill you.' And after Brixton had shut his eyes and opened them, Murray's smile was a little wider, perhaps too a little hotter and closer. ' But it would not be anything personal,' he said. ' And I do wish to assure you about that.'

Brixton was not deceived. This was it. He hadn't spent his years in Public Libraries, pulling down from the shelves heaven only knew how many books—he hadn't turned over thousands of pages for nothing. He knew. He always knew what he was talking about, and what other people talked about. He knew that often there was only a thin line dividing the man who was sane from the man with a problem. Although that was not what made a man a lunatic—it was not knowing how to handle his problem and never finding out. Nobody could say that sort of thing about Brixton. He had lent many a hand, handled much in his time you might say and that was the truth. People would be surprised. It could make him laugh to think he had handled a good deal more than people would suppose. But there was nothing to it, he meant it was of no importance one way or the other or whichever way you looked at it—yet at the same time very important, because it had meant he had solved his problem and so wasn't a lunatic like Murray Piper. Why, where on earth would he have been if he had had to go without his binoculars?

From that day he had been polite with Murray—but distant: in plain truth he had been badly frightened. He was not prepared to say he knew exactly what Murray's problem was, he could only guess. But whatever it was Murray didn't know the answer—well, throttling a man (or they used to call it garotting), was no answer. But what had happened remained in his mind, accompanied by fancies so vivid they assumed for themselves an independent life. Murray was not what he appeared: the reason for his being always dressed in clothes that concealed everything except his head and hands was that he was in fact a woman even though dressed to appear the opposite. Then too Murray was probably the kind of person who might do you a bad turn to teach you a lesson (like the virtuous thief Brixton had known who had haunted swimming pools to steal money from people's clothing—but only to teach them not to put temptation in other people's way).

It is perhaps a relieving change to say that nobody could have differed more from these two (and not to mention Mrs Trigger), than Clementine. By common village consent Clem was a darling. She was blonde petite and cuddly—and what more could anyone want who had an eye for what a woman could be? Also she was known as Smiler (although by some who consistently listened to radio serials this appellation was expanded to become the Smiling Widow with the eyes of cornflower blue). It was also a kind of wonder that by nature she was not wholly the sort of person which her soft appearances suggested. Insofar as there was any community life about the settlement, Clem was at its centre. She organized, but discreetly—so that nothing stuck out,

not by one small fraction of a mile. Despite all her charm it was
Clem who was aggressively indignant that the settlement had been
built without any thought for the difference a common room might
have made, a place where tenants could have met for tea cards
housie chatter what you would : there could also have been larger
gatherings with friends invited from outside : perhaps somebody in the news might have been invited to speak on some topic
of the day. And of course of an evening, and more especially in
the winter months, those who cared could have gathered to watch
telly—and so save on the power needed to heat their separate
units. Yet despite all her talents Clem had got nowhere, and
perhaps the charm of her appearances was all against her—how
could such an attractive piece of goods make herself into a
nuisance? Opposition from certain municipal councillors was
lumpish—males of a certain age and weight whose principal aim
in life had been to become ' independent ' (while living upon the
largesse afforded by industrial-slave labour and its products); who
would admit nothing in the way of responsibility or obligation
except what can be met by the payment of money (which one
inferred from concrete appearances was always in handsome
supply). And about all this Clem was not in doubt, for when she
had failed to engage the attention of councillors during daylight
hours, she had often without warning rung their doorbells at
night—but usually to find they were asleep over the box, or
boozed; and often enough, both. But at the time of the events
of my story Clem's social endeavours were at a standstill; and
for the big reason that at a certain late age of her widowhood she
had been knocked all ways by an attachment. In every sense a
sweet person, a bonus of sweetness had without notice or pre-
monition been added. And all this at sixty plus! It is not un-
common for people who suffer some disaster, anything from a
malignant growth to a tooth with a terrible abscess, to demand of
the universe at large that a question be answered, ' Why *me*? What
have *I* done to deserve? . . .' And it is implied that they resent
the visitation as unjust, and would much prefer that it should go
in the direction of some much more deserving person. But Clem,
grateful for her blessing, wished only that the whole world might
be similarly visited, whether deserving or not.

And yet, despite a high level of happiness, a from time to time lift to a higher peak of delight, Clem would remind herself that it was all so absurd at her age—which she never admitted to except to the pension people (but then what could she do about a married daughter and a grown-up grandson?) Nor could it have ever been foretold, no, not in all the creation of cats as it became her habit to inform herself. She had been fortunate in having a little money to spare, and having purchased a bed and mattress of more comfortable quality—well, who could have foreseen the strange consequences of engaging the services of a carrier to finish off the transaction. A great van had arrived one hot mid-afternoon, with the driver explaining that he was unfortunately that day without the services of his usual off-sider—a case of sickness, there was this stomach-bug going around, you want to look out lady. But never mind, he would manage with Clem lending a hand, no heavy-lifting, just a guiding hand around the awkward corners . . . And when all had been mastered, the man proving himself a marvel of skill strength tact judgment, anything that he delivered might have been just a feather bed—well, that's about it lady, and excuse me for saying now you ought to sleep sound . . . And (from her side), what about a cup of tea, let him sit down and it wouldn't take a minute? And there you are, that was it! A big strong patient man in shirt sleeves and wearing a stiff leather apron—not young, but his years a good way behind her own. Oh yes, overweight, but every cubic inch solid with honest virtue (and everything else apart it was all clear from his eyes, themselves transparently clear with every virtue you cared to name). Yes, oh yes! But was it to be believed? And yes, oh yes, yes it was, yes! But who would *understand*? Although for herself there was nothing she didn't understand, nothing she doubted— and the more especially all that she heard from red lips, soft and large, a little open and pouting; and just one item of a large and placid big-baby face. She understood too (how she understood!) that he took no liberties, she could depend upon it—that is to say until the day he did (and she did too without ever remembering who was the first).

It goes without saying that nobody about the village was deceived by the number of parcels Clem now took delivery of. There was seldom or never a day without: and not large parcels, although not small either—big enough to require the services of a

carrier, there was no question about that. And it may well have
been Brixton who was the first to notice it was always the *same*
parcel. He thought he might perhaps pull the carrier's leg. ' Hey
mate, it's time you gave that parcel a wash—it's getting grubby
with handling.' But merely to think of his joke was to be assailed
by a related thought. It was always the same parcel and no doubt
about it—yes, *but*! You always saw it going in, never coming
out. So what could you think? Only that daytime delivery was
just half the story: what arrived during the day was removed at
some hour of the night. Well, what business was it of his anyhow? Somebody might be breaking settlement rules, but he was
no pimp. And who was *he* to be talking when he had to be so
careful about his own arrangements? And that last was surely
the point—*everybody* had their arrangements to make: and so
very necessary to add that little bit of extra spice to life (and all
the more when nobody around these parts was under the age of
sixty). Without that spice your problem would get the better of
you—no answer, not a sign; and you became more of a lunatic
than you naturally were. Look at Murray Piper—look at the
MP!

But for all that there were more ways than one of adding the
spice. And so Brixton dedicated himself to solving the strange
question of the recurring parcel. Late into the night he would
watch, at first tingling with the lickerish excitement of confident
anticipation—until at last all was replaced by boredom as dragging
as he had ever known. All he learned was that there was never any
sign of the carrier, and although Clem never missed an evening
out she returned always alone at a sober hour. Nor did she ever
carry a parcel, only the small kind of bag which no woman is
ever without. So what?—and the next stage should have been for
Brixton to follow. But codes of great variety and nicety are
attached to all kinds of human activity. It may sound odd, but
Brixton had a curious thing about peeping Toms, a thing powerful
enough to deter him from seeing most of the new kinds of films
about which such a fuss is always made. A senior citizen (and
from an operative point of view that was to say a person who
travelled cheaply on the buses, and paid a cut-rate price for a
cinema ticket), he was familiar with much that appeared on the
latter-day cinema screen. But alas, his conclusions were unfavour-

able to film industry prosperity. He didn't know—but what was
the point in paying to be a movie peeping Tom when all as you
might say was nipped in the bud? And people who thought
different were ignorant. What did you see?— it was like watching
a picture of a boxing match, and every time a punch was all set
to land good and hard (wow!) the camera switched to some other
place: so at last you learned that promises would not be kept—you
would not be allowed to see what you had paid your money to see.
And so your money had been wasted. All that Brixton wanted to
see he had seen—but not on the cinema-screen. And there was
nothing in it, nothing much—it was just life, that was all. And
what you saw on the screen wasn't true to life, not by a mile. And
so it was all very tedious and boring (although he would admit he
had talked to a sailor who told him things were different in
California, where if you knew your way around and could put
your money down there were no broken promises). And what
it all amounted to was that it wasn't (perhaps wasn't much) in
Brixton's code to spy (not downright)—only if you were invited
to, or perhaps when people were hoping you would and would
be disappointed if you didn't.

It was because of Brixton's code that he never got round to
following Clem of an evening—and so he saved himself worse
disappointment than at the movies: for all he would have discovered was that her carrier (who answered to the virtuous-
sounding name of Whiteman, John Whiteman) had his van
parked at the quiet end of a neighbouring blind street: perhaps
only Mrs Trigger could have seen through its great sides with
picturesque scenes painted on—although it must be conceded that
Brixton would have taken a lively interest in a parcel that was a
sponge-rubber affair so weightless that unless tightly held it might
well have blown away on a windy day like a balloon: but anyhow, the sort of thing that needed only to be tightly compressed
to fit nicely into Clem's handbag (and if Brixton *had* known,
his satisfaction would have been much the same as when he
exclaimed over the right word in a difficult crossword).

But what Brixton would not have understood, was that no
matter how unlikely, Clem and her John were lovers in the truest
and most touching sense of the universal-saying—and that was
to say that acts of love were more in the nature of pledges than

ends in themselves. The pair were not strangers to 'all that sort of thing' (Clem after her child-bearing to a husband who had become a slave to the bottle: and John with his terror of a teenage son, the unhappy little boy whose mother in the agony of a 'mood' had tried to expunge herself beneath the giant wheels of a passing road-bus); but neither, and equally, had known until now that the tenter-hook ravages of hunger and thirst could be suspended without serious consequences, delayed and even assuaged by the ineffable joy of being within sound and sight of one who against all probability has taken up permanent lodgings in one's own heart.

It has yet to be mentioned that although the hillside settlement was plainly to be seen from many parts of the predominantly flattish suburb, there was a curious pretence that it was not what everybody knew it to be (as though people didn't say to strangers and visitors, 'Oh yes, that's where the pensioners live'). And all on account of an unhappy compound of pride and discomfort: on the one hand, 'See what we do for our pensioners in this country, all very nice and I am sure you will agree '—and on the other, 'Well, we all know that people who are old and not to mention poor have to be cared for, but don't you think all that rather rubs it in?' And it was probably on account of the latter view that although the visual fact was not to be denied, there had never been any practical attempt to create the cohesive community which the logic of appearances appeared to dictate. No doubt part of the trouble was passive resistance from the tenants, who in this matter may have rather resembled those Christians who do not deny they are in the world, yet see no contradiction in cherishing the superior notion they are not of it. But alas, as we have seen, one very practical result was that the Village (and a name preferred by the tenants to Settlement, although there were some now in favour of Court, a name which had lately been bestowed in other parts of the metropolis), lacked the amenity of the common room for which Clem had been such an aggressive propagandist.

But besides Clem in this matter of the common room there had lately become very active little Mr Hornley: and now that Clem was so much preoccupied with the personal planning which

stemmed from her new lease of emotional life, he it was who
would from time to time ring the doorbells of the borough councillors. And indeed, with Clem not at the moment in the running
it was as though Mr Hornley had set himself up as the village's
most conspicuous do-good person, a man not just dedicated to
persuading the authorities, but bent upon fostering the illusion
that the community-spirit aimed at had already been achieved.
And he provided ready support for this view by his daily assump-
tion of chores which ensured that he was brought into regular
personal contact with every tenant. It had for example become
his early morning habit to collect all the newspapers from the
wide main entrance to the village and leave one upon each tenant's
doorstep. There were mutterings (one morning there had come a
sudden heavy shower of rain, and those who had not been quick
enough had had a tiresome job drying out some very wet news-
print). But after all, if it was the exercise of the little walk they
missed, what was there to complain about? There were their
bottles of milk to be fetched—that is to say there were until Mr
Hornley thought of that one too. And some chore indeed! Well,
some three dozen and more bottles to carry and deliver! Yet soon
there were tasks even more substantial which Mr Hornley was
begging to be allowed to undertake—such as doing somebody's
washing (and such at almost any age is human nature, a boon so
unquestioned simply could not be permitted to go begging for
very long).

A top-heavy little man on short and meagre sticks of legs,
Mr Hornley was finally topped off with much coarse grizzled hair
which forever escaped from the confinement of a knitted woollen
cap. His eyes were so much buried in the creases of his forever
smile you could never be quite sure about their colour: but the
smile was often said to be winning. And perhaps true enough—
although you might at times wonder what exactly was to be won.
What you discovered upon closer acquaintance with Mr Hornley
was that he attached high value to views of life and universe which
he asserted to be his own: while he smiled he let you know that
it had been his long habit to think things out for himself and
come to the right conclusions. But often the trouble was that after
you had had the patience to listen you discovered that conversation
with Mr Hornley was like listening to somebody who had pre-

pared a very exact *résumé* of everything that had been printed in the newspapers over many years. Every variety of potted sentiment expressed in terms of press cliché was there, faithfully collected and preserved—and now displayed as a kind of touchstone whereby you might be shown to be thoroughly out of touch if you dared to question gospel-truth so self-evident and instant. But Mr Hornley's shop-worn sentiments were one thing, and his charitable actions were another: and although there were some tenants who were reluctant to accept them at face-values, there were more who were openly curious about his ' motives.' After all, it could hardly be said to explain everything that whenever Mr Hornley appeared at your open door and saw a teapot within easy range, he almost without your noticing it so to speak slipped inside to feel and discover whether or not the pot was warm. He liked his tea, that was the plain human truth of the matter: and maybe he liked as well to see inside your flat. But was the satisfaction of these two likings a sufficient reward for the chores he was so ready to oblige with?

And yet, whatever it might be that Mr Hornley in the words of a good many was up to, there was no denying that he had won friends and influenced many people about the village. Nor could it be denied that he was unique in having been inside every habitation with only one exception: Murray Piper had never allowed anyone inside except Brixton, and that disturbing occasion has already been mentioned. It was said of Murray that on one occasion he had spread his hands with his palms downwards as an apparent expression of distaste for the name of Mr Hornley. And by some his gesture was thought to suggest that he knew quite a lot about that gentleman but preferred to remain silent. By contrast it was Mr Hornley's readiness with a great variety of tit-bit information which had helped to win him his popularity. It mattered little whom you might mention (perhaps a nobody, perhaps at times somebody who happened to be featured in the newspaper) it would almost certainly turn out that Mr Hornley knew that person quite well—and if not now, then at some time in the past. Usually there would be a depreciating gesture (one accompanied by the smile nonetheless), one that rather recalled Murray Piper's handspread—but subtler, more ambiguous: among other things Mr Hornley was apologizing for being so well acquainted with people in the news: but perhaps he was also suggesting that people in the public eye could be a little suspect: and indeed the full implication of what he appeared to convey was that the most deluded people in the local world were those who considered themselves to be celebrities: any claims they might be credited with would be unlikely to survive scrutiny— and who could be more of an expert on any given case than Mr Hornley?

And yet, despite some suspicion that beneath a benign surface there might lurk an envious nature, Mr Hornley would be listened to with attention: by his accounts there seemed to be no denying that he had had an interesting life: and there were also times when what he had to say would compare very well with the more scandalous and titillating sections of the Sunday newspapers. Also, most interesting of all about his interesting life was his claim that among the many people he had known in the past about whom he could speak with positive authority, there was a handful now to be numbered among the inhabitants of the village. Not however that he was wholly imprudent in his gossip, and he would often say that for the most part his lips were firmly sealed. But he appeared to see no reason why two of these people should not figure in his repertoire of interesting stories and anecdotes: they were Mrs Trigger and Clem (or Mrs Rusling as her married name went).

Mr Hornley's account of his own life revealed that he had long been a widower, his wife having died suddenly from a mysterious illness never positively identified. It was all some thirty years ago. There had been no children, so he had at first found this misfortune a cruel desolation—until he made what he now called the sensible decision to enlarge his heart and broaden out his energies and affections into caring for the whole of man- kind in place of that one adored person. Those who listened were impressed by what appeared to be his sincerity and candour: he quoted scripture, about how a man who cares too much for pleasing his wife will tend to neglect some very important duties laid upon him by his Maker. But although the villagers were im- pressed by these sentiments it interested them more to hear about the nursing lives of Mrs Trigger and Mrs Rusling.

In the time of his working life Mr Hornley had been an insurance clerk who had never achieved any superior status in the Company he served, yet was much valued for the reliability of his work and conduct: his figures and his writing were neat and legible, he very rarely made a mistake: he was polite and helpful to policyholders, good-tempered and seldom on sick leave. Also everything that he owned, small house, furnishings, car, had been bought on time-payment without his ever having been late with his interest or a principal-sum instalment. What more could have been expected of him?—and the more especially when he resisted a show of militant policy in the clerical workers' union, and although claiming to eschew all forms of political activity chose always to vote against the Labour candidate in Parliamentary elections. Perhaps by some politically-conscious people he could have been conveniently written off as just another of the many conforming ciphers commonly met with in capitalist society: but by his fellow church-goers he was much respected for his resilient behaviour when he had suffered the loss of his wife: instead of folding he had accepted his change of fortune as a challenge, the very thing he needed to afford him the more abundant life referred to in the Scriptures he could always readily quote.

The word that might well have been expected to cover everything was Love: but Mr Hornley, who was nothing if not receptive to words and notions which became fashionably accepted, very soon substituted Caring. He did not quite say that everybody could without misgiving now throw away their Bibles—now that the sum of all the Past worthy of attention could be expressed in the newly-emphasized word: but what he did say was that provided you dedicated yourself to Caring there was precious little else in life worthy of your time and attention. And pragmatical, bent upon wedding action to belief with no delay, he had soon acquired the theory and technical knowhow required from a first aid and ambulance worker: a very nasty war was at that time fashionably in progress, and since males who could have taught him were in short supply he had been instructed by Mrs Trigger, brought back into nursing harness so to speak by this exigency. And anecdotes that she supplied remembered by Mr Hornley were remembered by many. Nurse Trigger was ready and bawdy with her wit, and as much addicted to putting on a show as would become familiar to the villagers many years later. ' I see you are handling that leg, Mr Hornley—but as my husband sergeant Trigger would say, make up your mind whether it is an articulated member of a male or female body.' Or, ' Pain? Well Mr Hornley, you don't remedy the disasters that inflict themselves on the human body without a modicum of pain—but perhaps I should say disasters that the human body inflicts upon itself. And when I use the word body I don't always mean people like you, Mr Hornley. No, perhaps a better expression would be human society.' But it is feared that Mr Hornley, devoted to Caring and always remembering the occasion, was not aware that rough gruff and ready old Trigger of the gripping and prodding great fingers had perhaps prodded an inch or two deeper into the mire of human affairs. Was it to be Caring? Or was it perhaps instead to be Justice? Was it to be trendy and say, If you drive don't drink. Or to say, Yes, *drink*—how do you expect to be able to face the traffic if you don't?

After theoretical and practical labours, awarded high examination marks, and presented at last with what he called his ticket, Mr Hornley had attended at Army Headquarters and offered himself for ambulance service. But only to be informed that his advanced years were not in his favour; perhaps it would be as well for him to trot along and see the Home Guard; or if he was at present unemployed the Manpower Office would make arrangements for him. And so it was that when his years were not very distant from the day when he would retire from his Insurance Company he resigned, receiving only a much commuted sum in settlement of superannuation arrangements. But to work as a Mental Hospital orderly was immense compensation: it was his religion of Caring come manifest and true. And it was during these years that Nurse Rusling (who in her own way of Caring had sought work in the institution so that she might remain close to her alcoholic husband), became the material for an anecdote which Mr Hornley would afterwards often relate: on the very day of taking up her duties Nurse Rusling had been shown around and introduced to patients by the matron: and on the very next day had been herself admitted as a patient: and although nobody on the staff had had a notion, not a soul right down from the doctors to pantry maids and handy man, many patients immedi-

ately declared they had known the previous day—and quite
positively.

Of course it had all within a day or two turned out to be a
mistake, or more or less. Under stress Nurse Rusling had suffered
a temporary collapse—so of course it was just an interesting and
amusing story, although one which if his listeners didn't mind
was to go no further (and perhaps Mr Hornley lacked the
sophistication to reflect that what had failed to stop short with
himself would be unlikely to behave differently with other people).
And of course he would never have said a word if anything in the
nature of a genuine mental sickness had been the story (and perhaps the man did indeed discriminate with his gossip, for although
it was well known to him that Murray Piper had been a long
time patient at the Hospital, Mr Hornley had never revealed to
the village this piece of inside information). And perhaps it should
be emphasized that fond though he was of providing you with
his unexpected and interesting sidelights, Mr Hornley was even
fonder of tirelessly relating the many particulars of his own sad
life-story : it was his great satisfaction never to spare you one
detail about the taking of his house property into which had gone
all that he could afford from a lifetime's earnings : the land had
been requisitioned for the purposes of a motorway and compensation had been inadequate (and plans for the motorway had afterwards been jettisoned anyway)—and there you had the true story
about how he had been sold a huge great pup and so come to
be ending his days in a flat of little more than large pocket handkerchief size. Fortunately however there was Caring.

No inhabitant of the village apart from Brixton had seen
inside Murray Piper's flat. But inside his head?—well, nobody
without any exception. And anyway, what would have been the
point? Except perhaps for an anatomist who might have noted
a few measurement variations. And that would have been about
it. And yet from what you heard it had occurred to everybody in
the settlement. ' I wonder what goes on inside that man's head?'
Nobody could say. With most people you knew *well enough*.
With the MP alas, you didn't know at all.

There are these days clever tests. Murray had had them all.
There are therapies which some people think valuable, and others

a load of rubbish. Murray had survived them too. And remarkably survived, because nobody could deny it—there he was at large, not on parole, a free man, responsible; a pensioner tenant who paid his rent regularly, shopped in the supermarket, cooked and ate food that nourished him; who put himself to bed and got up again—to survive another day which began with making his bed and eating his breakfast, and perhaps afterwards he would wash out a few things before settling down to . . . Well, it was what he did then, or didn't do, that made people wonder.

Not that he could ever be much observed by the laity (somebody in soft shoes walking a few yards into the wrong flat by mistake; somebody peering in through an open window on a summer's day when a washed-out curtain was hanging on the line).

But observed or not, there it was, he just sat.

How anxious disturbed and sorry are we to feel about the Murrays of this world? It is quite a question, but the answer long or short is unknown. After all there must have been times when William Shakespeare just sat: all that incomparable splendour inextricably associated with words, indissolubly wedded to all that marvellous and magical richness of language—was it all going on in his head? Perhaps, even probably, not. Perhaps without too much doubt he had to work like the devil for it every inch of the way. But work or no work, was there ever anyone to feel worried sorry and anxious about William Shakespeare?

Perhaps the chances are that Murray Piper had it much easier, at least to begin with. The fifth in an unbroken series of brothers he began to come undone only when the next in the family proved to be a girl. And yet, a placid child, never given to giving anyone any trouble worth the mentioning, he had not been conscious that his young sister was the preferred one until a day of Christmas gifts at the time he was entering his teens: a camera keenly anticipated (and according to his view, promised), had gone instead to sister Amy. And a few tears—but then his own new and shining gift was a bicycle: so no trauma, at least nothing on view to be readily detected. And was any bicycle ever such a consolation? Never! Nobody, not excluding himself, could have predicted it would make its contribution to disaster.

One morning during those same Christmas holidays, a morning

27

when summer weather had resolved itself into an unblemished
hemisphere of blue sky and crystal air—that morning Murray had
ridden out of town and turned off along the track that rounded
a leafy bend in the river. And soon he had leaned his machine
against a bank, hiding it out of sight behind the hanging greenery.
He wandered, and then he sat: all sounds and sights were there,
all the movements, birds that flew; water that slid and circled—
and glittered: the canopy of trees with the sun's living gilt on
leaf and twig—it was all a momentous delight!

But then as the boy sat he closed his eyes and made his momentous discovery.

*It was even better, and much better, when you had your eyes
closed!*

It took years, but he learned at last to dream with his eyes open;
and by the time of middle-age his dreams were much to be preferred that way. Because by that time the visible world never interfered, and never had a hope of comparing anyway. Also, what
was temporary, the world of the senses, was for the most part
shoddy. Cinemas, flats: not beautiful, not even pretty, at best
pretty-pretty. Cake-shop windows, coloured photographs—all
vulgar, like television, motor cars, advertisements in colour for
almost anything, take your pick, booze, women in their under-
clothes, striptease. There was nothing to compare or satisfy once
you had discovered and cultivated the refined delights of dream-
ing. And how very odd that the Good Book had been the true
begetter of it all! He didn't read it now, he read very little, being
in all things (and that included very specially his mental imagery),
his own authority: but in his little-boy days his mother had bought
at the door a large Book from a travelling salesman. It was called
*Grandfather's Bible* (intending thereby perhaps to signify the
sort of Book one's oldtime grandfather, believing and God-fear-
ing, would have approved of). It was selected and abridged, being
mainly from the Old Books (full of marvels and bloody cruelties)
—but the Book of Revelation could not be omitted, the jewellery
and the monsters were all there: locusts with the teeth of lions
and tails like scorpions, red black and white horses, serpents,
beasts, harlots: the light of lovely gems, jacinth sapphire emerald
jasper. There were many pictures, all engraved, and either by or
deriving from the old masters: the drawing was for the most part

vivid and wonderfully alive (or perhaps a better word in some cases was dead): there was Judith holding the severed head of Holofernes by the long hair: Isaac lay sprawled on a neat pile of firewood while Abraham his father raised his son-slaughtering knife . . .

In these latter days how vulgar cheap and sordid by comparison were the tinted harlots of the de luxe advertisements in the popular magazines!

Then the MP was nobody to be anxious about or sorry for? Was he then perhaps instead to be envied? Like William Shakespeare? Perhaps not. It was the rule of his dreams for people to be turned into monsters. And how many monsters simply cry out to be slain! But nothing personal, just on grounds of cool general morality. And as a change from monsters there was perennial pleasure—light and shade and colour, shapes flat or solid that glittered and made patterns. It was not important there was no comfort, no warmth, nothing human—that he had had to make do with a bicycle on that long-ago Christmas-holiday morning instead of the camera he had so much anticipated.

It was Brixton's view of himself that no saner pensioner inhabited the village. Well, you couldn't say for sure about some of the 'vegetables' (as that grim old faggot sometimes called them—Trigger: but you had to hand it to Trig, no flies on that old duchess): if there were people in pairs (*proper* pairs that was), or solo, who were neither here nor there, nobody in particular, just senior citizens, you saw them in busloads off to see the sights or play combined croquet and bowls with time off for afternoon tea and cakes, with a beer thrown in for the gents who preferred—well, a man shouldn't be uncharitable, but they were the sort that wouldn't wake up if you were up them. Well, never mind, leave them alone, a man only lived once, but nobody could say Brixton Brake hadn't cut his eyeteeth. As for other people, well, it was up to them, he didn't know but let them please themselves . . .

It was Brixton's habit, this talking to himself, a long monologue which reproduced the slang of forty years ago. Sometimes in the company of somebody younger he might for a change talk it out loud, tell about some bloke he had a snitcher on, or some joker

29

with the bad habit of poking borax, or he might work a slinter if you gave him half a chance . . . From time to time it surprised him that what he said was not understood—he might just as well have gone on talking to himself. All right, all right, nowadays there was a different lingo—and what was a man to make of it? Not so much the words mind you, more the way they came out. Or didn't come out. Mumble mumble. What was a man to think? Mumble mumble mumble. And what were the school-teachers paid for when they let the kids grow up talking that bad? Well, he might talk his own slang, always had, but nobody could say he couldn't make allowances—change over to suit the company he kept. Because damn it look at all those books on the Library shelves which he knew the insides of pretty well—well, of a good many. He wasn't ignorant—and that was the point: he had a suspicion a lot of these young jokers with their long hair-dos were—talked their gobbledygook (and they wouldn't even know the word) because they didn't know any different and never would . . .

And that was Brixton, sixty-five years ago named by his mother as a living reminder of the part of London she had emigrated from. And wearing his jacket of leather with cap to match, and his binoculars slung from his neck as always, he was off this high summer evening along the road that led to the Town Belt—that was to say a back to nature acre or so with a name that derived from many decades previously, when the city fathers as they used to be called had wisely decided that not every square foot of the territory they administered should be privately owned, either to be lived upon or for commercial purposes. And how things had changed! Nothing remained that might properly fit the descriptive name (although it had required the engineering of an Act of Parliament to put a stopper on the community benefits which patristic wisdom had had in mind)—nothing except the untidy token area already mentioned. And fierce complaints were endemic. Time and again it was promised that the thicket of fern and scrub would be cut and replaced by lawns flower-beds and open playplaces for children. Nothing had been done—and according to some there remained a convenient hideout for the misbehaviour of child delinquents. Who was there that didn't know? —half a dozen boys and one girl, not one among them who wasn't barely a teen-ager, and on their way home from school . . .

But it was surely much more interesting that this wasteland marked the point of change from a very old part of the city to the brash new suburb with its independent municipal control. In the city area there survived a strong urban mixture, rich and poor cheek by jowl, ample streets with giant trees and solid nineteenth century merchant-mansions (which had for the most part been divided up into flimsy makeshift flats): and around the corners terraces and lanes with the old wooden cottages where working men and their families had lived, but which were now inhabited by the less affluent middle-class with an infusion of fringe people —dropouts drug-addicts potters Polynesians painters people in television and journalism, a cross-section of the modern Bohemia. On the suburban side of the Belt all to the eye was uniform and conforming, the latest tar-seal serving the prosperous middle-class and their housing: new cars breaking the speed limit, a monstrous new hospital, the pensioner settlement—the vast new supermarket. And since this last attracted many shoppers from the city side, the Belt which it closely abutted offered a quiet and pleasant means of access with its traversing pedestrian pathway. But traffic was not all oneway, for pedestrians from the suburb went in the opposite direction to sit in the old roadside shelter which still marked the city tramway terminus of former times. From within the shade of this spacious building you had a splendid downhill view across tree- and roof-tops to the heart of the city; and then on the harbour where on a fine day anchored ships would be stuck in the glass of a glittering sea.

It was more especially on an evening out when he was headed for the Belt and the shelter beyond, that Brixton reassured himself that nobody in the settlement was saner than he was. Well, didn't it stand to reason? A man had two choices—he could fold, or he could say no damn it! a man only lives once: and with a roof over his head and money in his pocket, a theatre show to go to and books to read in the Library (and not to mention a bit of fun after going too long without)—well, what right had a man to complain? And to this end Brixton limited his gambling to one Ticket each week, and his drinking to what he could afford which wasn't much. And so he had provided for himself throughout what was now seen to be a long urban lifetime (except for an interval

many years ago when he had worked as a steward and had a look
about the world through a ship's porthole—and those were the
days when he had bought his binoculars second hand in a shop
in Suez). He had been content to remain in the city of his birth,
working for the most part as a warehouseman, and after his mother
had become a cot-case bad enough to be admitted to geriatric
hospital, preferring to live in a rented room rather than maintain
the tenancy of the cottage where his father, since the evening of
the long-ago schoolday when he had failed to come home for his
dinner, had never afterwards been seen. It was (and his constant
repetition), the condition of urban man—which he had read all
about in book-language in the Library. And the word was *read*—
it was from life you learned.

There was always a memory of his first warehouse—it was his
job each afternoon to see that a cage-trap was left ready on the
basement floor, baited for overnight rats; and an unusual morning
when he hadn't to run water into a washtub and drop in the cage
and its catch. But then one morning he fell down on the job, and
never knew about two caged rats until late in the afternoon. And
hurrying to be finished for the day he let them be until morning.
But it was then a startling surprise that now there was only one
rat! And deliberately he again delayed his drowning. That rat
reminded him of someone very close to home, somebody who was
learning to be up to all the tricks. Or else. It ended with his opening the cage door and leaving the creature to escape—because it
had guts that's what it had, so hadn't it earned for itself another
chance?

And all this was long before Brixton could remember hearing
talk about the rat race.

What in his old age it had all added up to was that it was not
much in Brixton's nature to suffer from doubt and indecision,
from scruples of no-account. He used his head (as he frequently
told himself); no pensioner could get by on the official money,
so it was up to a man to see himself provided with something
extra, although not by any means foolish or risky—robbery or
violence or blackmail, they were out. There was a thing he always
remembered about his long voyage and those many ports of call—
people need never go hungry so long as they had something they
could hire out or sell (and wasn't it one of the rules of the rat

race?) And where was the harm anyway? Being grown up was
not like being a kid, when you didn't have to have money to have
your fun: being a man you knew that for city people it was the
rule for money and fun to go together: everybody knew that, and
it would make a nice change if some people would go and shut
their mouths! . . .

Halfway through the Belt Brixton veered a few yards from the
pathway to remove his cap and unsling his binoculars. These
objects he concealed beneath the greenery which overgrew an
old tree stump. He used a coarse comb on hair which proved to
be thick brown fuzz: his appearance was transformed: his
masculinity was perhaps a little diminished, but his sallow skin
helped to suggest that he had become a kind of honorary Polynesian. And after he had taken off his jacket to turn inside out
before putting on again, the Islander touch was emphasized—
for the reverse side of the leather showed a satiny mother-of-pearl
sheen which closely matched his silken shoes. And the long and
short of it was that Brixton had for the time being remarkably dis-
carded appearances familiarly known about settlement and suburb.

With daylight still around it was a little too early for many
people to be in the neighbourhood of the old shelter: but city
lights would be turned on soon now, and already fairytale lamps
were travelling about the harbour waters and wavering through
the mist left over from the afternoon heat.

It was Mr Woolly's customary evening and there he was, ahead
of Brixton as was customary too, and seated in the shelter-corner
one thought of as his. Brixton was vain about knowing this
superior quiet-looking senior citizen: tall, with snow-white moust-
ache neatly trimmed, there was no question he was class; nor were
there any of the signs you might well expect in a man of his years
—no pot, no dragging feet, no red sagging eyelids, no drooling,
no food stains, no neglected fly-button. On the contrary! And
Mr *Woolly*! That was the name he had never appeared to be
offended by since the evening Brixton had brought it out in conversation (and a name told him by another shelter acquaintance
who had said as the old gentleman passed by, 'Old Woolly!
You want to go and take a look at him in Court some time.')
Brixton had supposed he might be a lawyer; and after all, the

C                              33

passing intimacies of a lifetime had included a good many he thought of as professional class : schoolteachers doctors clergymen, and these days smart young men who dressed in the fashion and might work on a newspaper or in broadcasting. It was remarkable too that never since the evening when Brixton had introduced himself had the pair been short of things to say; and all the months of their meetings appeared to make no difference at all. Brixton's head was such a repository of Library learning anyhow (and he had besides a memory for bawdy stories, and more especially those which would often amuse by pointing up the comic differences between people of the Old Country and the Antipodes : and there was the good one about the pommy gentleman farmer who had taken his cow to visit a neighbour's bull, and afterwards described the service as tophole.) Then too there was that *word*—and Brixton knew that Antipodes meant opposite feet, and so must let you know that he knew. He explained—see? And for his part Mr Woolly, speaking in sentences precisely put together, would tell of happenings he had noticed about the city. Why, just one day ago, he had seen a young woman who was about to enter a bus and first she flattened out her patent pram so that it would fit into the outside luggage rack only a few inches above the roadway : but the extraordinary thing was that without any appearances of misgiving she had left her baby sleeping in the contraption. Well, she appeared to be a young woman of intelligence, but perhaps she had no imagination : well, you know, just think of it, a sleeping infant deposited there to travel so close to those terrible fore and aft wheels.

And the discussion that followed besides rapidly passing away the time occasioned some heat. Because Brixton began by saying he didn't know—and then declared that the young woman should have been prosecuted. And Mr Woolly had said, yes, perhaps : but the difficulty was to know how exactly to go about any such matter. It was almost certain there would not be any legislation which said in so many words you were not to put babies in the outside carrier racks of buses. Well, perhaps there was some regulation to that effect but he would doubt it. No, proceedings would probably have to be on grounds of an action which endangered human life : and yet it might be said in defence that the baby had safely arrived at its destination, it might even be shown that the child

34

was peacefully asleep upon arrival. Yes indeed, there could be
difficulties. But Brixton despite another assertion that he didn't
know became positive. You couldn't tell him, he said. And he
said it all went to show what you could expect from a woman—
although, mind you, he had known some women who were different. But by and large a man was lucky if he managed without
ever letting a woman get the nips in—and he had known a good
few jokers who had let themselves in for all the works. Got
married to proper bitches. (Did Mr Woolly know the story about
the two dogs?—they met down the street and one dog said, ' You
don't look too good on it what's wrong?' And the other dog said
well, it was the little bitch he was in the habit of knocking around
with, just at present she was giving him hell and he felt miserable.
And the inquiring dog said he was very sorry. ' You know,' he
said, ' I've often thought that, haven't you?—aren't bitches
women?')

Mr Woolly smiled at the story: he said it was clever, but it
did women an injustice. Where would any good man ever be
without his own good wife? And he went on to speak with pride
about one of his own clever daughters as he had several times
done before. She was his favourite daughter, but for many years
she had successfully established herself in London: she was a
scholar, an authority upon music for the harpsichord, and she
taught in one of the Royal Colleges. But alas, there seemed to be
very little chance that she would ever return home—she said that
after so many years there would be little to interest her at the ends
of the world. And Brixton said yes, but there were too many
New Zealand people who went overseas and got big ideas. Poor
old Enzed!—sometimes he thought it might be just as well if it
was called Small Beer. Now as for him, he had seen the big world
once—and he began to tell all over again about what he had seen
of it through a porthole . . . But for the most part Mr Woolly was
not to be diverted from some comments about bringing up a
family. There were trials and difficulties in marriage he would
agree. There were constrictions, there could be narrowness, but
perhaps all was compensated for if there were affectionate children—after all, he said, that was what we all needed. Just plain
affection. Yet the world did not understand that old people did
not need it less, indeed a great deal more . . .

It was more or less their usual conversation this summer evening, boring to neither—how could time have passed so rapidly if it had been?

Mr Woolly stood up first, taking from his pocket a posh brand of twenty cigarettes. Brixton murmured his thanks and slipped the packet away out of sight: he did not need to look, knowing that inside a slit in the plastic wrapping there would be a small envelope: and inside that two five dollar notes folded over. Always he was grateful. He began, 'Mr Woolly, I could lend you a hand, it's up to you . . .' It was the formula: but his companion gestured. 'Thank you, not now, another time.' There was warmth in the pressure of his handshake, and afterwards he turned back to say, 'I expect my wife will shortly be away on a visit to our son and his family in the South Island. You must come and visit me one evening, we can be at our leisure. But for the time being we must wait and see.'

And returning, resuming his usual monologue along with his more usual appearances, Brixton was thinking. It had been a pleasant companionable evening, profitable whatever way you liked to look at it: from his reading he remembered the words, 'common denominator:' he had not been certain that he understood their meaning: but suddenly now he found himself pleased and grateful, enlivened and warmed by a sudden quick rush of understanding.

It would not be untrue to say that Mrs Trigger secretly thought of herself as the boss of the entire village (would any of the vegetables have wanted to claim the title anyway?) But a discreet woman with her tongue, thoughts of grandeur never showed much, and her boss status might well have remained a guarded secret if it had not been for her benevolent practicality. There was almost nobody upon whom the fruits of her magnanimous activities had not been visited, cardigans scarves slippers bedsocks the lot. And she had listened patiently to a thousand complaints about the pains (for the most part rheumatic), and pangs (the ingratitude of sons daughters and other kinsfolk), of old age. There was plaintive mention of benefits conferred and never appreciated or even acknowledged: and sometimes Mrs Trigger wished for some show of the manliness which was so signally her own characteristic

—but what hope? So she knitted—and knitted, and clicked her tongue, and was sorry and sympathetic and said so. And apart from the knitting there was one other practical benevolent thing— she kept an ancient stock of old-fashioned medicaments, homeopathic remedies (belladonna, nux vomica), besides a selection of out-of-date materia medica (senna pods, tincture of myrrh, ipecac, slippery elm) now almost totally ousted by the new chemical therapy. She kept also a stock of bandages and aseptic dressings for use in case of accidents, but was often a little brusque and off-hand about cuts and wounds she judged to be trivial. After all, she had all her long nursing experience; and after marriage had cared for Trigger, in health matters a great baby who was always imagining some fatal hazard—it might be a scratched finger or a sore throat, a stomach ulcer or a pain where he supposed his intestinal vermiform appendage to be.

It should go without saying that rarely did it occur to village sufferers to suppose that Mrs Trig could herself be afflicted by any of the illness accidents and phobias which they so often and so unfortunately found themselves targets for. Nor was it known to anyone that no matter how much kindliness and caring she concealed beneath a gruff manly mask, her secret reason for being grateful for the high situation of her flat with its comprehensive view was the opportunity this advantage afforded her to watch over the day to day fortunes of the MP. And how fortunately odd that the pensioners had taken up those initials and made them stand for Member of Parliament—when because of peculiarities they might as readily have signified Mental Patient. Was Murray aware that by the strangest of chances the sister who had defeated his Christmas hopes of a camera was living not many yards up the slope? Who could know? But it was perhaps unlikely—after all, Trigger, the name had been acquired during the first years of Murray's incarceration when he neither knew nor cared to know what went on in the world apart from his very own day to day interior events which were incalculably more absorbing (and despite the impossible-to-describe agony of pain which often kept them company).

It would be an exaggeration to say that Mrs Trigger suffered great perturbation of soul over the fate of the brother whom she thought of as the odd-colt-out of the family—that is to say, as the odd one apart from herself (although she had in fact long since ceased to think of herself as an oddity). Perhaps her own especial drive had been short of some necessary ingredient or lasting quality: a long time ago she had suffered over the young and pretty blonde probationer—true (and where was the little powder-puff to be found now, and how little she cared!) Afterwards until there was Trigger there was nobody—or almost nobody: she could more or less remember, count on her fingers the more or less number of times, opportunities to share the bed of some nursing colleague: there had been moderate pleasures, no regrets, and perish the thought, no guilt. (Or would it perhaps be some-thing worse?—a sense of no-importance?) And was it perhaps on account of this sense that she had come down on the side of Trigger? Alas, he had been no help at all. But anyhow, there it was—her ' problem ' was not important and she never thought about it as such. Trigger was gone, soon she would be gone her-self—it was perhaps remarkable that Murray hadn't gone already. She thought of him as one of the colts—and what nonsense! He was like herself, old pack-horse. Only perhaps, disguised.

Perhaps the important point about it all was that she had coped. She would have had to be less than human not to be concerned about her brother, and the chance happening of their being located so close to each other in their old age. But that didn't alter the question—why hadn't Murray coped? Who, once arrived at a stage beyond false and sentimental notions common to young people, expected that worldly affairs would necessarily work out in favour of individual hopes and desires? But then wasn't there a sense in which the pair of them had been bedevilled by the extraordinary caprice of fortune in favouring nine other colts? And whenever this last thought entered Mrs Trigger's head she would shrug her shoulders, perhaps fling down her knitting while she made herself a cup of tea. All those people were *too much*! Who could cope?—remember and properly distinguish among nine wives, not to mention tribes of progeny plus a variety of good paying occupations posh houses station wagons enamelled boats and so on? It was all a long long way from being a favoured little sister and a target for so many expensive birthday presents. And yet Mrs Trigger would have been at any time prepared to swear that for herself, she was *not* bedevilled. No regrets, no envies—

cross her heart (and deep in that same heart, very private, a wicked pride: she could see straight and face facts, so where was the answer to the nagging question?—Why was her brother, a man of the same blood, a weakling?)

It should go without saying there was very little about the open and verbal Mr Hornley to remind anyone of Murray Piper— and yet Mrs Trigger would often be visited by the thought it might perhaps do *him* a world of good if somebody would take him by the shoulders and shake him. 'That man Hornley!' she would say. And it was then a prolonged meaningful silence (or at times a downright statement about a thorough good shaking).

No doubt prejudice had had its beginnings in war days when the little man had received from her his first aid instruction. But all that might perhaps have been forgiven and forgotten if it had not been that with his bandages and sterile pads he would often compete with her in ministering to tenants who had suffered lesions: there would be cuts bruises varicose ulcers eczema (although the word now was dermatitis). And it was to Mr Hornley's credit that, knowing himself to be more or less an amateur by comparison, he had the good sense not to edge in too much on the professional Mrs Trigger—preferring sometimes instead to extend his ministration to people about the neighbouring streets (who had heard about prompt service with all competent appearances). And so Mrs Trigger had been much placated: and all might have been well if it had not been for a few pensioners so insensitive to atmosphere that they let it be known they *preferred* the attentions of Mr Hornley. And that was an insult Mrs Trigger could not swallow, nor would any understanding person have expected her to. And then again, although Mrs Trigger would often say many sensible things about the village set-up, agreeing about the crying need for a common room and approving of Mrs Rusling's campaign, Mr Hornley would at times earn for himself more of her dislike by his insistence upon some amenity or piece of decoration which she might consider quite uncalled for, besides downright eccentric. It was his view that when the suburb's gardens for the most part abounded in a variety of painted ornaments (gnomes who sat on toadstools and fished, a great variety of animals, huge wooden sunflowers), it was shameful that the

39

settlement's great open green spaces boasted nothing of the kind (and surely an unpleasant deprivation additional to the restrictions upon the planting of shrubs or the keeping of pets). For compensation Mr Hornley had lately retrieved from the borough tip the frame of a rusted little tricycle—which he then cleaned and painted before fastening upon the saddle Algy, a ventriloquist doll of his own making. Algy sat with feet on pedals and hands securely fastened to handlebars, a cheeky smiling urchin wearing a blue woollen cap with a bright orange tassel: and Mr Hornley saw to it that his ornamental position about the open spaces constantly changed so that appreciation might be from every possible angle: in times of bad weather Mr Hornley would see to it that Algy was taken in out of the rain.

It did not please Mrs Trigger that she appeared to be the one exception to a rule of universal love for Algy.

It was about this same time too that Mrs Trigger was especially put out that Mrs Rusling seemed to be availing herself of Mr Hornley's first aid services; nor was it a help that in her view the Rusling woman tended to be 'insipid' when the village verdict was virtually unanimous. Sweet! Well, a little ball of a blonde widow who carried on with the great big-baby (the thought was distasteful, but she would not deny that for size he was to be compared with Trigger), the dropsical carrier with his absurd regular parcel! (But although Mrs Trigger was not a less perspicacious person than Brixton, she was additionally more spontaneously imaginative: and so she was not plagued by Brixton's compulsive itch to secure exact knowledge which, while satisfying curiosity, might at the same time excite much in the way of lecherous imagery.) Who cared a fig what Rusling and her big boob-blob were up to? And how short of what they *were* up to would the imaginings be of many a less mentally bright person than Mrs Trigger.

But it is true too that Mrs Trigger could with justice excuse herself a good deal of rancour by reflecting that unless there was a doctor in the background, Mr Hornley might be attempting to handle something that could be very tricky. She did not know the exact nature of the Rusling complaint, but according to rumour it was perhaps nothing of any great account: it was nonetheless arrogant of that pompous little man to suppose he could safely

meddle when his qualifications were so slight as to be little short
of ridiculous. Why, she could remember the case of a *trained nurse*
who had failed to draw conclusions from a sudden rise in temperature, and complacently continued with methylated spirits and
sterile pads when the patient was rapidly dying of a violent infection which could have been checked only by the use of an anti-
biotic. And another curious thing was that Mrs Trigger had heard
the story about Mrs Rusling's having been a nurse-cum-temporary-
mental-patient—and was now in a mood to dismiss it as gossip.
Because after all, if she was a nurse why was she allowing the
Hornley creature to dress her sore leg? Despite her butter-
wouldn't-melt appearances was she underneath it all a thorough-
going loose woman? And it is perhaps likely that Mrs Trigger's
abhorrence of Mr Hornley's practice of first aid on behalf of
Mrs Rusling was not wholly grounded upon concern for that
person's welfare: it is unlikely that anyone in the world could
have elicited the admission, but perhaps the truth of the matter
was that she was jealous: perhaps too the little male horror was
himself a lecher. Once in her life long long ago Mrs Trigger had
found the world a transfigured place simply because of the presence
in it of a pretty-pretty little probationer nurse. All had come to
nothing: she had had brief acquaintance with transfigurations of
a slighter character—and eventually she had made her decision
to make do with Trigger. But forget? No, never! And now, very
curiously, there had been more than a little to remind her in this
slight and truncated blonde widow—and sometimes to such a
degree that she would find herself visited by a very sudden, very
sickening nostalgia. No, she told herself, and again NO! And
yet perhaps the history of this little retired nurse should be in-
vestigated. But then she remembered; Trigger you old pack-horse,
she told herself. She had her reputation to sustain—it was much a
part of her popularity in the village that she had her head firmly
screwed on the right way. And although this was a public view,
it was a matter of some pride that it was also private truth. To
live, to love, to lose—it had all been known to her—on the pulse
and in the bone. She *had* her head screwed on the right way—
repetition would have been quite impossible, the final agonizing
evil.

And yet a powerful appetite for damnation is human. Mr

Hornley was meddling—and so was Trigger: meddling with her own emotions. Why did the blonde Rusling encourage that insignificant and deplorable man? (And the word insignificant was a giveaway, because there was a sense in which Mr Hornley was powerfully the reverse—and that she was obliged to admit.) But even so, why?—when the blonde was or should have been exclusively wrapped up in her carrier? And if that great comic lump had had a grain of gumption he would have wrapped his lady friend inside one of his own parcels and departed with her for keeps, so solving what appeared to be a private problem blown up to the size of a settlement scandal.

Seen from the outside, Clem's affair was at first view a comedy, modern surely, perhaps black—but perhaps it could also be seen against a mixed background of what was tragic romantic and comic in the traditional sense. Mr Rochester had his wife in the attic, a grim business indeed with for the long time being no solution in sight: but you had to risk appearances of heartlessness and laugh—while at the same time reassuring yourself there was a glimmer of hope that emanated from the plain little duty-captivated governess. And so it had all turned out, conveniently assisted by a fire that salvaged while at the same time it maimed and destroyed.

What was the analogous solution for the carrier (John Whiteman, the man with the thoroughly virtuous-sounding name), and for his Clementine? There was fire already, but it had so far remained confined to the heart—where it raged without destroying: consumed, yet was never short of fuel; was assuaged, without affording any sensation of salvage. There are those who wish to be saved from the appetite or the passion that possesses them, but Clem and her carrier were not to be numbered among them: certainly they had no wish to be maimed, nor were they: on the contrary, it was a major sensation that they had been made into a perfection of wholeness. Yes, yes, all this—but then nobody could have been more wretchedly aware of the imperfections of time and circumstance—the van furtively parked, the termagant wife crippled and disfigured after her monstrous encounter with the wheel of the juggernaut bus, the delinquent son with his destructive rage (and all the more terrifying when it presented to the outsider frozen appearances of control which could badly deceive even the official observer with his reputation for 'expertise'). What had all this worldly evil to do with a man so far removed from extravagant behaviour of any kind as John Whiteman?—a man who could be vouched for by all who had known him over many years as patient generous obliging honest, a thoroughly good-natured man. And in his late middle years he had had the unforeseen good fortune to meet with another of similar kind. Identity had sought out identity, and so without fuss or fanfare the sum of sweetness was doubled; the clear light of perception had been stepped up to become a dazzling illumination. It was as though without pushing themselves forward for selection the pair had been chosen to inhabit the Earthly Paradise. Or if you prefer, as two simple good souls in harmonious relation they could be seen as a working model of the sort of thing a Humanist might talk about in abstract terms.

Who at first could believe the news that broke one morning when Clem was found on the floor beside her bed—with a slaying knife thrust so deep that only the handle showed?

## II

With the village set upon its hillside and plainly to be seen, no inhabitant of the suburb could fairly claim not to know it was there. But apart from the expected visitors (friends and relations, welfare workers, Christian believers committed to acts of impartial charity, besides sectarian propagandists—Jehovah's Witnesses, Latter Day Saints), the balance of traffic was pretty much in favour of the enveloping suburb. Pensioners must eat. There were some, true, too old too tired or too deformed by the misfortunes of rheumatism and what have you for any kind of excursion. For some, a few, there were meals on wheels: others phoned their orders to the supermarket—for the white plastic loaf, the packet of something edible for which you paid the fancy price of cellophane and fancy printing in pretty colours; or for the neat tin of vegetable food with its label-promise of carrots potatoes green peas and other green vegetables according to season: and all presenting to the eye a stiffish paste, salmon-coloured and nearly flavourless (or you might prefer the same sort of thing with a tang of meat—but except that the mixture was a little darker and the label spoke as well of onions and a cereal there was nothing all that different).

It is true that the man on the supermarket van delivered to the door, and there was another man who once a week hawked his hen eggs; nor must the post-girl be forgotten, who came as far as the main entrance—where the ranked letter-boxes suggested an enterprise for the battery rearing of bantams. Very occasionally there might be a gala day with flags, with bowls of flowers on trestle-tables and cups of tea and plates of cakes: perhaps a visitor from overseas, and afterwards a speech from the mayor (it was considered very fortunate that anniversary day for the opening of the settlement coincided with New Year).

45

But on the many many ordinary days the flow of traffic you noticed was mainly out, not in.

Ah!—but now there was the excitement of sensational hours when all was reversed, when the plainclothes men came and no pensioner wished to be absent: or if the bobbies of any description went they soon returned—and with offsiders, doctors some said, or they might be fingerprint men, or experts who could make decisions about murder-weapons. As for the uniformed constables they were never absent for long, one always on the doorstep of Clem's flat to stop people from entering (and yes, even those who very positively asserted themselves to be the closest friends of Mrs Rusling), one at each entrance to the settlement, and one more to be about among the crowd and keep an overall eye.

And besides a great mixed bag of pensioners' friends and people from about the suburb there were the press reporters—and all very friendly and easy to talk to. Because who knew?—you might have something newsworthy to tell: this is to say something that hadn't already been told, and not once, perhaps a dozen times over. Because very naturally it had quickly got about that Mrs Rusling, Clem, had been found stabbed to the heart: and there were many to say they had seen all with their own eyes long before there was any kind of policeman in sight: all was described, the blood that had made a great red patch on the carpet, and had streamed in broad red streaks from the place right above Clem's heart where only the handle of the death-knife showed. And some remembered—more than one had been wakened by noises in the night, others had heard footsteps, and some could not have been more certain there had been somebody about with a torch. And there was a bright young newspaper lad, very eager to prove himself a media-man to be reckoned with, and he made the bad mistake of taking himself off to the nearest phone before he had secured for himself any check at all upon his harvest of gossip. His paper was first with the news, a few lines in large type—yet a chilling account of what certainly appeared a shocking affair. But alas, the news item proved to be totally misleading —and this despite its being at one and the same time visually accurate and a powerful exercise of the imagination. For it must have been about the time when the scoop edition of the paper was being hastily shoved into the honesty boxes that the doctor

46

(turning up late, but at last), wiped his cottonwool across one of those bloodstreaks—to say almost immediately the 'blood' was some kind of mixed substance, probably greasepaint (the smell of perfumed tallow was a giveaway). There were exclamations. There was surprise and scepticism. But the doctor settled the matter by knocking the back of his hand against the knife-handle —and knocking it over! It appeared to have been tenuously fixed into position with that same alien substance. A few more wipes and all was clear, no wound, skin unblemished, no knife-blade. Beyond all question Clem was dead, and that was the first certainty; the second was that she had not died from the thrust of any slaying knife.

For quite some days after the first sensational press reports there was very little news, only routine matter about expectations of a post-mortem report: it appeared that it might be an indefinite time before accurate information about the cause or causes of Mrs Rusling's death would be made public. And because of much that was mysterious and bizarre, with overtones many people said were sinister, a continuous (and for some of the more nervous pensioners), a comforting police watch was maintained at the settlement. Meantime the plainclothes men were kept so very busy that to assist them in their inquiries a little square tent was set up bang in the middle of the only little bit of level lawn: a roster of pensioners was prepared, and one by one, or sometimes in married pairs, they were escorted in to sit and enjoy the pleasure they felt in being considered important people with important questions to answer. There was however remarkably little to it— there were strenuous endeavours to prolong moments of importance, but it was soon pretty clear that nobody could (or was willing to), provide those trivial-seeming items of information which might turn out to be useful. But simply nobody, as Detective-Sergeant Clive Ringer said to his superior, Tups (although formally, Detective-Inspector Tupsall).

As anybody could have foretold the two men were much informed about Mrs Rusling's carrier—the regular and frequent delivery of what all described as 'her parcel.' The two officers made their appropriate notes, but it was all more or less a waste of time: already they had had their long talks with John White-

man—who was in any case well known to them on account of
several serious misbehaviours committed by his difficult son.
Already they were so much impressed by a character who appeared
to be so transparently truthful that he virtually ceased to be a
person to whom any suspicion could be supposed to attach : despite
their being experienced men even his virtuous-sounding name
impressed them : and it was, if anything, even more remarkable
that they did not suspect his plausible emotional behaviour to be
a put-on job : it was hardly to be believed that men well accustomed to a variety of emotional display, and so much of it
spurious, could have decided that in this instance they witnessed
the genuine thing : and yet, so far, that was the case. The man
might have the appearances of a great blubbery overgrown baby;
yet movingly, there was nothing false about his resolute attempts
to restore vision by ridding his eyes of flooding tears with his
great outsize fists : not at all—and the younger detective was even
a good deal concerned about the risks he appeared to take of
gouging out his eyes. And there was additionally the man's terrible
problem—the wreck of a wife to engage another man's sympathy.

But then of course all might well depend upon what the cause
of death was shown to be : and after that the affair could hinge
upon the question whether or not it was to be considered an outside or inside job. And in the meantime Tups inclined to the first
possibility.

'That boy, now?' he said. 'Well, *there* could be something.
These young hounds,' he said. 'Lumps of cold ice if you ask me,
broken bottles, well there you have it. Callous killers to a man—I
mean to say, kid!'

But his offsider was doubtful. They would have to wait, agreed.
But look, to his view an inside job. Well, they must wait, but see,
this was no affair of broken bottles. Sophisticated—well, ask yourself, it was that sort of thing. The rubber handle, well work it out
for yourself. It tied up with the movie sort of thing they showed a
lot of these days. It was psychological—it could be anyone,
granted, but what about some old psychopath? Male or female—
or something in between?

The older man was not much interested in the sort of pictures
which nowadays were supposed to entertain you—well, something
to take your mind off your worries, that was what he hoped to

see in return for the money he paid (and my God, could Ringer remember back to the days when the price of a ticket could be a shilling or less?)

Tups was a senior officer who would soon retire. He dressed for the part in the dark three-piece style of a decade ago, his hair a shade longer than you might have expected was his only concession. He had been in his time very much a family man: he had kept his fingers crossed—and thank the Lord the kids had all grown up *clean*! And all safely married now with half a dozen pocket-editions to show for themselves. All good kids, both generations—and far too many bad bastards about the world these days. Spare the rod—there was a young hound just the other day, and another of the cold-ice breed, a sexo who had talked back, quoted somebody (parson or priest, so he said) who had laid it down, twice a week—to keep a man healthy. Well, personally (but just between you and me), he wouldn't disagree—but that didn't mean a man could go and take the risk of killing to get it! Even for a married man there were plenty of times when he had to wait, the wife couldn't always be expected to turn it on.

For Ringer it was sometimes a bore (when it wasn't amusing) that poor old Tups had his hang-ups. Not him, not Clive Ringer. He belonged to the times. He was very happy to be a member of the Film Society (where he had had the good fortune to meet his pretty young wife too), and where he was in any case well placed if limits were exceeded (films that were too blue—and a description which always reminded him of the telly seen through somebody's window at night when curtains had been forgotten). Not that he would have minded, he meant personally: he had no hang-ups of his own so far as he knew. Why mind about what Tups called sexos—well he meant the 'consent' kind, leave the queers alone was his motto, except for the odd one they were harmless—they could always make you laugh with their camp talk, and very generous with drinks. But not a bit of good trying to tell Tups (and what do you know?—sometimes he had thought there was something about old Tups: in his old age: well, never mind, but the thought *had* occurred to him). It was safer to recommend Cliff Richards—and think of that! Or prod him into going and seeing a picture he would enjoy (without going and having a word with the management—or writing a report to *his*

D                    49

senior officer). And perhaps the differences all came out in their different ways of dressing, himself with his loose collar and tie, jacket on his arm no matter what the weather—and it could be the most serious creed he had ever subscribed to (years ago he had wavered and nearly made a big decision, and maybe it could be true that he had never *quite* got off the hook after the big Billy Graham mission)—there was no greater actor that had ever lived than Rod Steiger!

Because cause of death was so long in being established (and after all it had to be remembered that it might eventually be shown that Mrs Rusling died of heart failure or some other 'natural cause'), Tups made a concession to his colleague. Inclining to believe that the victim had probably been poisoned, he for the time being dropped his notions of an outside job in favour of investigating Mrs Trigger. After all there were very few villagers who hadn't spoken about her medicine chest, and some too had mentioned her useful stock of pads and bandages for cases of accident. There was also her readiness with a variety of woollen comforts, and it appeared a good-hearted busy-body—but they would see. Then too, when Ringer passed around a list of tenants just in case there might be a name which rang a bell, there had been a youngish uniformed sergeant to whom the name Trigger meant something. In camp during the war, an infantry corporal, he had had for his immediate superior a man of that unusual name (and believe it or not, Hair Trigger as a rule—ha ha). He remembered an occasion when his sergeant had invited him home on weekend leave—to meet his wife. He remembered that on the way they had called in for a quick one and Trigger had drunk more than was good for him—and it all ended up with a rumpus while they were eating their dinner, some kind of a dispute, and sergeant Trigger had made things worse by calling his wife 'stable-bred.' Well, sharp words—and he remembered because after that Mrs Trigger never allowed anybody a word in edgeways: told all about how she was brought up with the horses her father bred—although not to mention a tribe of brothers: her dad ran a stud with a world reputation or so it was claimed—and yes, he remembered now, name of Piper . . .

And then the two men focused again on the list, because it

might be a coincidence but there it was, a Trigger yes, but also a Piper . . .

And Mrs Trigger, sharp-eyed over discarding stitches which would make more shapely a current tea-cosy, but having it politely put to her by the man in charge, Detective-Inspector Tupsall, was not at all averse from asking the two men to step inside. But alas, they could not observe that conversation and questioning induced in her any visible reaction which might be thought unusual and never to have been predicted: nothing tell-tale, certainly not. Although to begin with, and until Tups sharpened his tone a little, she was much inclined to wander from what he called ' the subject.' It was however her reaction to permit herself her own sharp remark that she was well aware of the subject—the subject was a dead body: and observing keenly, she was pleased to note that the policemen were themselves visibly inclined to shy away from the subject. And then as though a hat had been dropped she was off again, denoting with a wave of her hand that of course they might look inside her medicine chest—and go ahead, what were they waiting for? It went without saying she had nothing to hide —well, wasn't she a trained nurse with a lifetime's experience and hadn't they already been told? And now an irrelevancy—as law-enforcement officers what did they intend to do about the traffic? Speed noise fumes and engine soot. Everybody on the road at the bottom of the hill was breaking the law—and every moment of the day. *Dead bodies*! *Breaking the law*— and that was where the dead bodies came from. Thirty miles was the law—and she had to do her own shopping, and how was she to manage? And the entire pack of them full of booze into the bargain—and what did the law say about that? And it all reminded her of years ago when she was a girl—then it was floating around in the air in those airships with armchairs pot-plants and sofas. Give her back the horses any day you liked—and *then* there wouldn't be any of this talk about breaking the law! But anyhow, they were wasting their time talking to her about dead bodies . . .

But perhaps not altogether.

Although it was not their investigation of the contents of her medicine chest that breached the defences of Mrs Trigger. (What do you think you're looking for anyhow? You don't suppose just because I'm a trained nurse I keep a select range of streps and staphs in there do you?—and anyhow, all that's out of date. Old hat. It used to be a streptococ-eyed world when I did my training —and now it's all virus, very fashionable. And as you'd expect with all the new words kicking around, nobody to know what they're supposed to mean. Virus. I know why it's popular, I know—it's because people are ignorant. Virus—they think it's to do with virility, hair on the virile chest, and virile biceps to bust any ribs they wrap themselves round).

Ringer hadn't a notion about the word homeopathy; and Tups, although he could remember something vaguely from a long way back, was no better off: pathy—well of course that meant something bad, something morbid, well there was pathological. But homeo—he couldn't be sure: the spelling was a bit different, but could it be the same as that other word—which meant a man of morbid sex? And since Ringer couldn't help they took away the entire contents of the chest after each little bottle had been listed, with a description of its contents accurately copied from the label. It surprised them a little that Mrs Trigger appeared indifferent and made no objections.

It was not until they were at the door that Tups put his question, delayed until this moment.

'Mrs Trigger, according to our information, your maiden name was Piper. Could you tell us whether there is any connection by way of family or marriage with the man who occupies the flat alongside the one where Mrs Rusling lived?'

And now after a shadow of surprise and a moment's delay the reaction was as explosive as anyone familiar with the lady would expect. Yet not in the least what the two men had hoped for. Nothing guilty—on the contrary, an aggressive righteousness which failed to carry the stamp of a cover-up for guilt.

Mrs Trigger was marvellously indignant. Well, who was she to deny what they could easily go and find out for themselves! That was to say if they didn't know already! But that wasn't the point—and anyway, what had it got to do with Mrs Lecher going and getting herself bumped off? If she had?—and if you asked her nothing at all. And just because Mrs Lolly-pop of a certain age had it coming to her what had that got to do with other people's private lives? And if there was any meddling she knew what she would do—write to the Minister of Police. And if that did no good go higher, write to the Prime Minister. And she didn't give a razoo whether they knew already or they didn't. And being the sort of people they were of course they would go and find out—only now what she meant was about how her brother had been a mental patient for many years. But then he'd recovered —so hadn't he the right to live his own quiet life just as he pleased without any interference? And if she liked to live close by just to keep a watching eye on somebody who belonged to her own flesh and blood—and mind you, *without letting him know*, then what had that got to do with them or anyone else? Who could know what harm they might go and do if they went and told her brother Murray his sister was living nearby, a next-door neighbour? Why, before they knew what they were up to the shock could put him right back in the hospital after all the years— and just let them think what *that* was going to cost the country when there he was paying his rent and getting along quite nicely on the age benefit so long as he was left alone . . .

Tups when he could get a word in was reassuring.

' Mrs Trigger . . . in the meantime . . . I assure you . . . Well, there was . . . in your own words Mrs Trigger . . . a dead body. Well . . . but in the meantime . . .'

She appeared to be placated, perhaps reassured; and the two men had passed nearly out of sight before Tups decided well, *now* it was time for the day's last card.

As they returned up the hill there was Mrs Trigger at her o.p, her wide-open window, and knitting (although if you observed carefully, a little fumblingly), her tea-cosy.

' We won't come inside,' Tups said. ' But I thought I should let you know—the victim, the dead body as you say, was like yourself, a trained nurse. She began as a probationer in . . .' He could perhaps the better observe her reactions if he pretended to consult his notebook for the date and name of the Hospital. ' Yes, he went on, ' here we are, yes, her maiden name was Barrow, Jessica Clementine Barrow.'

It said something for Mrs Trigger's character, not to say the character of her toughness, that although Tups and his colleague were not on the whole disappointed, there was not much (and perhaps indeed, very little) in her reactions which might be useful

if and when there was a case to present before a jury. All it amounted to was that before she had been instant and talkative: and on
this last occasion she had had nothing to say. You might have
said too that her features remained dead-pan—except that having
put her knitting down, with her elbows on the window sill, she
brought her hands together in a pointed arch in front of her face
as though she was saying her prayers: and the suggestion of
prayer was reinforced by closed eyes and lips that moved. Well,
there you were, a jury was always a jury—which was to say the
trouble was you never could tell, so much depended upon what
you could get away with. And apart from the exceptional case it
was the general rule that nothing was likely to turn out well for
the dramatic touch when shot through with melodrama—which
in a court atmosphere stood too many chances of being shot down
as far-fetched. Paperback fiction and thriller films were all right
in their place; but in court there were pressures coming from more
than one direction to remind the jury that courts of law are not
places of entertainment: despite the public appetite for thrills
there could be no truck with the heady excitements of what was
imaginary.

And meantime, while there remained the unanswered question
of the post-mortem report (it appeared the medico best to be
depended upon had been away on holiday, hence the delay), the
two officers sat down together to recapitulate and decide whether
or not an inside job was still to be assumed. Well, Piper—and
close attention was surely and shortly called for. But then what
about the male busy-body, Hornley? And that was not to mention
Brake, and the man with the forename which invited you to suppose he had perhaps been inside—or if not then perhaps it was
time he was (and indeed, it seemed that a uniformed man had
a line—there was a suspicion about Brake because of loitering, it
seemed he was a too-frequent men's-cottage-visitor).

So now then, where were they? The post-mortem delay was
frustrating, and the more especially when there was the double
thing—who in the name of heaven and all the saints had 'joked'
with the knife-handle? Somebody around the bend?—and surely
that would point in Piper's direction.

But it was decided that in the meantime they would go and talk
to Hornley.

Now the sad and disturbing truth of the matter was that since the discovery of poor Clem with grotesque theatrical appearances of having been murdered, nobody about the settlement had been feeling more miserably guilty than little Mr Hornley. And he was forever repeating to himself, 'For no reason!' It had been his mission in life to care—and for everybody! Care! It was his philosophy and should always be spelt with a capital letter. And who was there to say he hadn't practised what he had preached?— although let it be understood that he had *never* preached, for it was a first principle that preaching had no role to play in a life of Caring. And so there was nothing about the dreadful Event which afforded him any true ground for self-reproach: and yet, in all the popular excitement there had been a thing which he might fairly think to be monstrously unjust. It was well known that hardly a village soul had neglected to inform the inquiring detectives about Mrs Trigger's medicine chest, besides (although with much less emphasis) her generosity with knitted comforts: some too had mentioned her first-aid attention to accidental burns bruises and scratches. And yet, so far as Mr Hornley could discover, nobody had had one word to say about his own good deeds: officialism had had to wait to hear from his own lips an account of his delivery of newspapers and milk, about the training and qualifications which entitled him to offer his own first-aid services —even about his bestowing upon the community the gift of the decorative Algy.

It has already been mentioned that when Mr Hornley was in a mood for gossip, he seemed not to understand that it is too much to expect a secret which he was himself failing to keep, would be kept by persons to whom it was confided: and it would seem to be another defect of his understanding that when a dead body appeared mysteriously on a village doorstep so to speak, he failed to appreciate that Mrs Trigger's medicine chest would take on larger dimensions in the popular mind than day to day matters of village routine. So what it all for the present amounted to was that Mr Hornley's Caring, and the lack of appreciation it had received, was much connected with his feelings of guilt. After all, he had cared, not just theoretically, but in the effort of practice—and now all had gone wrong. He could even secretly charge himself with having failed to afford the poor dead woman the protection it was clear now she had needed: he hadn't saved her from disaster, and what he *had* done, of meagre account now it could be seen against such a monstrous sum total, had for all that not been appreciated: even worse he could suspect the almost impossible—that it had hardly been noticed.

So who will be surprised that it was Mr Hornley's present passion to co-operate with the police? He must endeavour to compensate for his illusory guilt: for the time being he was filled with a determination to uncover the culprit.

But when the detectives put to him their questions, the two of them seated comfortably in the two easy chairs of the tidy cared-for living space of his flat, nothing turned out like the interview he had so many times rehearsed in his mind before the knock came on his door.

To begin with it was some surprise that it was already known to his questioners that Mrs Rusling had worked as a nurse in the hospital in which Mr Hornley had worked as an orderly: but more to the point, it greatly surprised him that she was also known to have been briefly committed as a patient. It was also disconcerting that, looking forward to the luxury of forgiving himself (for having done so little when he had known so much), he found himself as it were freshly accused: for a moment he had the prickly sensation that perhaps he had a good deal more to forgive himself for than he had reckoned on. And from that moment on there was no delay. It was an unusual experience for the two detectives to be themselves disconcerted. Who could have supposed that anybody so meek and mild would suddenly assume appearances of overweening assurance? For all their professional skill, try as they might, their interruptions and objections were ignored—or else peremptorily disposed of while Mr Hornley, with a fluency which failed only for occasional want of breath, assuaged his guilt over not having cared nearly enough.

Nothing was withheld. They heard about how he had done his best—and what man could do more? Did they know, did anyone know—what was concealed beneath the varnish of affluent society? Well, he could surprise them with the cases he had uncovered. The public didn't know—but then it didn't want to know. He knew of old people shoved into any old corner—and so long as they were out of the way who cared? He had had a bad case on his hands not very long ago, an old man with bed sores, he was dead now lucky man, he had lived in pain at death's door for far too long. And until you looked you could have no idea of the bed-sores. The old chap's sheets were clean—and you couldn't altogether blame the relatives: after all, a hospital case, and what were anyone's hospital chances these days? And after paying taxes for a lifetime the only way to get hospital treatment was to stand out in the road and let yourself be run over. Hospital beds were all filled with people who had been salvaged from the traffic smashes. And that was another thing—when it came to traffic smashes what was to be said for the grown-ups who smashed up their children as well as themselves? And the hypocrisy—you only had to look at the figures, *news* when somebody was kidnapped, and *statistics* for the thousands knocked off on the roads, besides kids that included babies in arms. Why—

Tups, who occasionally wrote a reminding word in his note-book, was trying to interrupt, wanting to know whether the old man with bed-sores had been a villager. But not a hope, and it didn't matter—for by this time Mr Hornley had finished with outside cases: now he was talking steadily about his life and good works in the village, talking indeed about the early hours of the day of the dreadful discovery. And of course the two men had heard it all before, more or less, during the time of their questioning in the little tent. But never mind, give the little man his head, you never knew what might turn up, give a man enough rope . . .

Well, he had slept badly, one of the hot autumn nights they'd been having—a close dark cloudy morning and much too early to get up—well, for another half hour. And too early for the newspaper-job. But then he had lost a lot of sweat in the night and felt he was due for his morning cuppa—and bad luck! Not a drop of milk! So he got cracking—and well, you know, Mrs Rusling's door was open—well! And it was now that Mr Hornley smiled his rare *other* smile. Usually his face was creased (his eyes buried in the creases) with the forever smile which suggested to some people that it was put on fresh each morning, almost you might say a piece of daily personal furniture like spectacles or false teeth, and no more to be done without than his knitted woollen cap. But then too it was a smile which was also a mask, one moreover made of wood—so that, always exactly the same, you seemed to be informed that it told you no more than you were entitled to expect. But this was one of the rare occasions— the wood had gone, and what it had been replaced by was saying, Look, there must be some mistake, there are no reserves at all! And perhaps it is true to say that nobody would ever understand unless they understood that with his *other* smile Mr Hornley believed that however much he might seem to be giving away, it was nothing of any real consequence whatsoever.

Perhaps the point is clear if it is said that Mr Hornley always used his unusual smile to accompany mild feelings of guilt about petty weakness he secretly believed would thoroughly endear himself to you: it was from the smile of wood you might suspect anything at all—and more especially that it might be as well to be careful if you engaged yourself in any kind of dealings with Mr Hornley. His temporary smile was now accompanying his statement that it was not too dark for him to see that the front door of Mrs Rusling's flat was open—and always very fond of his cup of tea (he would admit that weakness), thinking that her pot might perhaps at that very moment be warm, he had paused at her doorstep for a discreet inquiry.

'Uh hu?'

Well nothing! Not a sound, and surely none of his business! A hot clammy night. Ventilation, a breath of air. Or she might have gone out with her milk bottle last thing at bedtime and afterwards forgotten to close the door. Or she might have had company? . . .

And now he remembered (and his face had by this time securely resumed its wooden smile), something he had forgotten, he meant at the time of his tent interview—perhaps it had been because he had had to wait so long in the queue: he had missed out on his mid-morning cuppa, and that always sent him into a flap. Well, while he was doing his errands with his bottles of milk the idea of a harmless little joke had come into his head. Algy! Why not? Why not put Algy on Mrs Rusling's top doorstep, looking in so to speak—as though wanting to ask a question? Hey, what's going on in there, lazybones?—time to get cracking! It would be something to remind the lady not to be so careless another time, goodness gracious, going to bed with her front door wide open! But then, do you know?—after two cuppas with the early morning news turned low, and when the newspapers would certainly have been delivered, well, it was the strangest thing, the first thing he noticed! There was Algy still on the top doorstep, *but he had been turned round the other way*! He faced out, not in, as though he had just now emerged from the flat on his bicycle. Well, chores had to come first (although when he arrived at Clem's place he said uh hu all over again). Only louder. And nothing! But he was sensible, he reminded himself, Chores first, then this must be looked into—but in the meantime he shifted Algy out into his usual place right in the middle of the square of lawn alongside the big natural rock which according to people who were supposed to know was probably a better bit of natural sculpture than you could be lucky enough to find anywhere in the country (although there were other people who said it was just rude) . . .

And Mr Hornley would have said the superfluous remainder—about how the egg-man, early that day, almost before people had finished their breakfast, had looked in through a corner of Mrs Rusling's bedroom window not covered by the curtain and—

But Tups was sharp and peremptory with his interruption.

' Answer carefully, Hornley,' he said. ' Is there anyone you would think likely to handle that Algy of yours—I mean apart from yourself?'

For the two detectives it had been a disappointment that no finger prints had shown up on the rubber knife-handle; nor had anything much been derived from a careful check upon numerous objects about Clem's flat. And indeed, you could conclude that nobody had been in and out of her flat much (although there were a few clear signatures which it was not anticipated her honest carrier would want to question).

In up-to-date language Tups had said to Ringer, ' Fingerprint-wise we get nowhere.'

And suffering that day from stomach-pains Ringer had observed that many things were these days accounted wise—you might almost say it was wonder-wise that humanity wasn't more sign-wise about something millenium-wise about to arrive any minute.

But then he quickly agreed that truly finger-prints had got them nowhere—and at the same time reminded himself he must be more careful not to insist so much that his language was a cut above his superior's (although nobody who could appreciate an actor as good as Rod Steiger was going to be satisfied with the second-rate).

Ah, but now! It turned out there were plentiful tell-tale markings to show that Algy had been handled a good deal more than might have been supposed. And it was Ringer who said well, very revealing, even a bit pathological, as though the lad had been marked for life so to speak. Only a doll, but he had encountered pressing advances from numberless paederasts of both sexes. But Tups was as usual impatient with observations of this character.

'Whether this one or that had a hand on the boy needn't concern us,' he said. 'What comes right up our alley is that Piper had.'

But Ringer found this jubilant tone depressing. It was true that along with the finger-print information there had been a result reported from the team of younger men who had been raking over the most likely area of the suburb's rubbish dump. A few commonplace household items, vegetable peelings, fishbones, plastic wrappings, an empty toothpaste tube; and all bundled together in sheets of newspaper—but along with them too a fragment of white paper smeared red, with the printed word Leichner, and the number 3: and perhaps better still, wrapped in gold paper, the slight remains of greasepaint, colour red . . .

Ringer could anticipate and see Tups right on the ball, saying, Mr Piper tell me please what brand of toothpaste you use: and whatever the answer might be, taking the appropriate empty tube from his pocket, saying now here we are wouldn't this be it? And again that morning he felt himself as though breathed upon by a sudden sour wish to deflate.

'Chief,' he said, 'I could be speaking out of turn—but just where does pinning the stage murder on Piper take us? I mean mightn't that line turn out to be a tactical mistake—I mean say he's a lunatic (if you will pardon the old-fashioned name)—suppose he decides to come clean (and it's my hunch he might be delighted to). After all, what's the point in going right out after the missing Toyota when it's the Realota that would be news?'

Tups was preoccupied, and pretended not to notice Ringer's wit—until at last he said:

' I think you could be mistaken. With some people it comes to exactly the same thing. I remember when I was a lad—my father was running a small-town pub, and it was just before the talking film. There was a touring show, *Uncle Tom's Cabin*. I went with my father, and I never forget the old coal-black slave—he was very pally with little Eva, a paleface angel with curly golden hair. But nothing in it believe it or not. But the old man got whipped to death by a man called Simon Legree—and if ever there was one, a proper bastard. Well anyhow, there was a party at the pub afterwards for the players, and the mayor of the town invited. Well, what do you know?—his Worship refused to shake hands with Simon Legree, left for home in a tremendous stink. Blow me down if he hadn't taken the stage show for real.'

And all Ringer could think of to say, was, ' Okay, Chief!'

But Ringer had been right. Murray Piper was (if nobody minded the old-fashioned word), a lunatic.

At his opened door he smiled, said he had been expecting a visit and they were very welcome: he wanted to assure them in advance he had nothing to hide. But then why did he ask them to remain on the doorstep while he made a few ' adjustments?' For, leaving them at the wide-open door, he as though invited them to look in while he hastened about: he tidied, adjusting a cushion, removing a thread from the carpet, closing the books that were open on his table—and then going at last across to his kitchen to reach for a tea-towel which he used to cover the books, besides what looked like a mass of untidy written-over sheets of paper. And afterwards, when his visitors were seated on his long and threadbare couch, he sat at the table to push the tea-towel aside: he took up the top sheet of paper, and appeared to read to himself with grins and chuckles while his free hand spread itself protectively against their by any chance reading as well. But again there was a sudden change as though it had been decided this was no occasion for privacy after all—what was on the paper revealed nothing (and that was perhaps to say no part of himself that must remain private and guarded). He read aloud, slowly and with relish, rounding the vowels, making the consonants snap and hum, trying as it seemed to extract every ounce of savour from the words:

> *Jesus put the kettle on*
> *God make tea,*
> *Holy Ghost do buttered toast*
> *And bring it all to me!*

It was Ringer who spoke first (Tups might be a lapsed Catholic, well more rather than less; and for any kind of Catholic the Holy Ghost mightn't cut much ice compared to the rest of the Holy Trinity; and not to mention the Virgin; but for all that he was in no doubt about this sort of thing, it was blasphemy): and Ringer was amused, he was even charmed—well, what was the point of being with-it, a member of the Film Society and all that if it didn't bring you into touch with something you had missed? Something odd and striking with a touch of spice—well maybe you could say highbrow spice: and it had been Ringer's discovery this last needn't always be sex (after all there were times when you could have too much of a good thing).

'Yes,' he said, 'very good. It's a good laugh—but you know I think I've heard that rhyme before.'

And Piper's reaction was extravagant, almost not to be believed. He hurried to push his piece of paper beneath the untidy mess on the table—and then it was more than a spread hand: *both* hands, yes, and his body spread as well, right across the table.

'You mean it got away! Oh, no! I'm always so very careful— I can *allow* that one to escape—now! But never until now, never! But you are lying, I know it!'

The heat of his freckled face and red hair was troubling—as though he would in a moment suffer the fate of Dickens' Mr Krook and die of spontaneous combustion. And the workings of his face, with the tears starting—ah yes, they were troubling too.

It took fifteen minutes and a pot of tea before he was smiling although still tear-marked—and by that time the two men had improved their knowledge of this kind of behaviour. It was not to make sure that the words of the rhyme were not seen that he had spread hands and body—no, to prevent their escaping of their own accord from the paper on which they were written. It was insanity.

But all that might have been a fruitful beginning to a revealing conversation proved to be a disappointment. In careful detail Murray Piper began to recount what he described as the story of his life: and like all such accounts with far too few exceptions it turned out a tiring bore. Explaining that people of his psychological type, despite some opinions to the contrary, were very reliable and truthful, he demonstrated by recalling that on a particular day (after several attempts he identified the day as a Tuesday, and not after all a Wednesday), he had had an egg for his lunch (but no, he remembered now, it was a piece of luncheon sausage), and then he had decided to walk into town (he was at that time living in lodgings on the far side of the city)—but no, now he remembered he had taken a bus, and it must have been an absent-minded day because he had taken the *wrong* bus, and never realized a thing until he was some distance on the way. So to save time (or to be more exact, to make up for lost time), it had meant a taxi, and of course it was wartime (and he apologized that he had forgotten to tell them), taxis were scarce—although not for the soldiers, and well, yes, what he really meant were the Yanks. Besides paying a high price they would engage a taxi by the hour, with them it was money to burn. But where was he, how far had he got?—oh yes about walking into town (and it was a Tuesday, yes, remember it was a . . . No! Now he remembered, it was . . .)

There appeared to be no point in it, not a thing which would be worth the time it took to decipher: Ringer was beginning to yawn when Tups judged the time to be opportune for the first serious question. ' Is this? . . .' he began.

And it was. That brand of toothpaste, yes. He took very great care of his teeth which were all his own, which wasn't too bad, now? Well, not for a New Zealander, would they agree or not? There was a time when he had used a dentifrice—but scratchy, he thought, not good for the enamel. But what a shocking business, the state of the country's teeth! What they were doing for the children was beyond praise, although about fluoride he was in two minds—

Tups interrupted, putting to him the question of the remains of number three.

And yes, indeed. Stage make-up, number three. Carmine, and as well there was number two and number one. Sometimes you could build a better colour if you used a bit of lake, no number—and none for vermilion either. He asked for the exhibit, smelling it and making a face. 'Gone off, do you think?' he said. 'They make them from animal fat, clean tallow,' he said. 'But perhaps it goes off if it's kept too long.' He smelt again, and a sudden beatifying smile broke on his face as he reached to put the stuff under Tups' nose. 'Yes,' he said. 'Get it?—yes, it's still there, that perfume, it's elusive—they say it's one good reason why people get sold on the stage—once you're hooked you can't leave greasepaint alone.' And handing back he said, 'But no good for fresh blood—it's better to use cochineal with toilet paraffin or glycerine. It glistens.'

It was as though Tups, timing excellently, his tone a model for situations of gravity, came in on cue.

'Mr Piper, it was number three you marked your neighbour with. Wasn't it? Mrs Rusling? Now wasn't it Mr Piper?'

And it was as though Murray had himself been cued. There was his pause, silent and pregnant, while he opened his eyes wide and arched his eyebrows: it could have been that he was trying not to burst out laughing.

'Well, of course!' he said. 'Well,' he went on, 'it was my responsibility. After all, the many many years I had known her—you could truly say a whole lifetime! Don't you agree there was a responsibility? I am very proud that I rose so splendidly to a sombre occasion. There are facts in life we must all face, although I do admit this one was unexpected, something I had never forseen. Well, you know, living next door to one another like that—and I *knew*—and I could never believe she didn't know too. And then what was fate up to that morning when I woke up much too early feeling restless, and couldn't resume my sleep. A sticky night, perhaps you remember, I had meant to throw off my eiderdown and I forgot—and by the living jingo I woke up all of a muck of sweat as Oliver Goldsmith has his grand young lady of fashion say. And my mouth was very dry. I thought, Murray boy, what you need is a nice cup of tea. I said, Come on Piper, no slacking! Up you get! Now! Go and fetch in the milk without waiting for that stinker. Pardon me for saying what I should not say, but the man Hornley is the stinker I refer to. I do not like him for my own reasons—but it is no secret that once, many years ago, he was set up in a little brief authority over myself. It was during my time as a hospital patient. I did not like his authority— he was kind in all that he did for me, but he left me in no doubt he had authority, and that my own authority must be subordinate. I pretended to agree, but I hated him—because his authority endeavoured to crush my own, and I believed my own superiority made me as superior as he was. If there had been any convenient means I could have killed him—and it would have been the right thing to do, because when he had me at a disadvantage as a hospital patient I could not have been blamed if I had asserted the absolute right of my superior authority. It might be said of me that I was a madman, but that was to my advantage because it would be said I was not responsible, and so I could not be punished. I would have proved my point, risen to my undoubted right and responsibility to assert my superior authority without having any penalty inflicted upon me. So—'

But Tups, taking the risk, had intercepted.

'No, Mr Piper, listen carefully. We want you to tell us what it was you knew, and couldn't believe Mrs Rusling didn't know as well.'

During a silence which began to be embarrassing Murray again arched his eyebrows, but this time it was not as though there would be a burst of laughter.

'I have nothing to hide,' he said. 'It was my responsibility. It was dark but I saw the door open, and the doll on his bicycle was looking in. And I thought my Kiwi thoughts if you understand— Hello, hello, I said to myself, what's going on? I thought, we are not on speaking terms but she is my sister and I have my responsibility. There was a time when I had wished her dead because in the hot time of youth the heart is proud and vulnerable and does not submit when demands and desires for first place are not any more to be gratified. And yet she was kind to me, as well in the time of my growing up as when she nursed me in hospital—when her looks had grown so far out of all my recognition that in all that time of my illness beyond all hope of recovery I never knew her for my sister. Nor would I have known that my sister had followed me here to live alongside, if I had not

E                          65

one day by chance in a city street met one of my many brothers who very kindly did not persist in his questioning whereabouts I lived in these latter days. But he told me instead it might interest me to know that according to report our sister, for many years a widow, was reported to be living in a new slap-up place for pensioners. It did not please me to hear this news and know that my sister had been following me about. For whenever thoughts of her would enter my head I would think again how I had wished her dead—and now once again I was ridden by that thought. So when on the dark morning I saw the door open and the doll looking in, I thought now perhaps was the time for all to be understood so that with a good heart all could at last be forgiven and forgotten. I told myself that I had surprised the doll in the very act, and for certain his intention had been to enter the flat and destroy my sister. But I had intercepted in time and would save her, and because I had acted upon my responsibility all matters that had gone wrong would now at last be put right. And all would be forgiven. And so I did not hesitate. There was my torch in my pocket and I entered with the light searching—although not for long, for there was my sister on the floor in her nightclothes. I was too late. I knew she was dead before I touched her, but I touched her to make sure and she was cold . . . And then I returned to my own place for my number three and that handle . . .'

It was Ringer.

'Would there by any chance be another cup of tea in that pot?'

Tups was aware that Ringer's trouble was uneasiness over silence of an uneasy kind. There was nonetheless his faint gesture of disapproval—for neither of them would now ever know whether or not Piper's next words might or might not have put the matter neatly into the right kind of nutshell . . .

While Murray made a fresh pot he chattered. It was during his hospital years that he had developed his useful skill with make-up. In the Christmas season there had been parties charades little plays—once a pantomime . . . And he had turned the doll the other way round so that he might have the proper appearance of being the culprit.

A few corners from the settlement there was a sign from Tups,

and Ringer turned the big car into the quiet blind-end street where
it had been John Whiteman's habit to park his van. It was another
close autumn day, very hot in the car and the two men sat silent
and slumped—although not relaxed, instead fidgety and on edge:
perhaps one could have said they were feeling cross, perhaps a
little guilty. After all, how in the name of? . . .

Again it was Ringer.

'Okay, okay chief, same here, silence for whipping cats.'

But then his thoughts wandered as they so often did when he
was behind the wheel of a car. Although it had to be a big car,
plenty of power. Power, the kids on their bikes had it between
their legs—but too obvious, a bit crude. But still, power. Putting
you into motion and the whole world was doing it. That, and
watching telly. And with one or the other while you were at it
you couldn't do another damn thing (except for the kids, but
again, too crude). A whole-time job doing nothing and the whole
world at it. Ah, but there *was* another thing. Dreams, you could
dream—and the whole world was at it. And that was it, dreams
and power—who could wonder about the 'accidents'? Or
mind? They were just incidental parts of a world composed of
dreams and power . . .

It was not for nothing that Ringer was a member of the Film
Society.

'Two smart cops. Okay chief, okay. With just one thought—
about how they went for a fast twosome up the garden path.
Okay, so the pair of us sell ourselves a mare's nest. How do you
plead, Ringer?—I plead guilty, sir. And no extenuating circumstances? Well, not really. And now I am speaking for myself—
honestly, I'd love, chief, I'd very much love to see you extenuated
while remaining a no-hoper on my own behalf. But count up to
ten before you say whether you agree or not—it was the bloody
melodrama that sent us on that fast walk. Come on, don't be
coy—it was the bloody lunatic that turned us into a pair of clue-
searchers. When there's nothing in it, not one bloody thing, the
woman had a heart attack, it's as simple as that. There's nothing
in it, never was, never will be. If I get what I deserve I deserve
to be demoted. So what?—there are times when I would *prefer*
the routine of uncovering the disappearance of utilities and
laundry vans . . .'

Tups answered with another sign, and the car turned out on to the main road: in seconds they were well beyond speed limit: it was mutually understood that top priority was an unscheduled overdue hospital date.

# III

There was talk that Mrs (or as was sometimes said by people with sharp tongues), old mother Trigger was not any more to be seen at her window. It was as though the destinies of the village were not any more to be presided over by its great earth-mother deity.

There were some who wondered about her knitting: many had benefited, and some had thoughts of a repeat: a few, very few had never benefited, and among these were Mr Hornley and Brixton. Well, Trig had never concealed her disapproval of the little man's amateur bandaging: the withholding of favour from Brixton was perhaps more difficult to account for—but then he was *especially* favoured by his reception at her window, and her showing no signs of impatience no matter how long he engaged her attention. Despite her being no great reader of books herself, it was not her habit to change the subject when he spoke compulsively about information derived from another new library book. And it was on a day when he was full of statistics (birth-rate, with ten times too many people already in the world: and food-supply, with the corollary of an impending all-too-terrible disaster for mankind), that he approached her window despite her not being publicly visible: and while remaining stationary in her easy chair, although overflowing its boundaries, she had beckoned and asked him to go to her door and enter. He had never been inside before. It surprised him that she was not knitting, but bringing with him a mindful of up to date information nothing else for the time being was relevant. She embarrassed him a little by keenly watching his face while she remained orientally silent with folded arms: and when, having exhausted his first subject, he was about to move on to another, she interrupted.

' Mr Brake,' she said, ' what you tell me is all very interesting—

69

as they say, that is for sure. But today I have not asked you inside to hear about a shortage of edible matter to put into a surplus of mouths. No. I have not myself in all my lifetime contributed to that surplus (which I often see loitering about the streets, and that is not to mention schoolchildren on holidays when I sometimes think the best kind of tactics could be a machine-gun). Nor if it comes to that did I ever make a contribution to the supply of edible matter—well, shall we say in any primary fashion? Trigger my husband never had any complaints about my cooking that I am aware of, but in the days of my maidenhood the livestock I grew up with was not in this country regarded as suitable for human consumption. Horses, Mr Brake. Beautiful creatures, Mr Brake, I love and recommend them for loving. But I am running on ahead of myself Mr Brake, because a moment ago I intended to suggest that unless I am much mistaken you are another one who has made no contribution to the surplus on two legs. Homo sapiens, they say—and it sounds like a good reason for the surplus, Mr Brake. A man with his supply of sap can be a great nuisance—and I believe there would not be a woman, I mean with experience of the married state, who would honestly want to deny that I am speaking a red-hot truth. Now then, as one of our prime ministers used to say, and like myself, Mr Brake, you are of an age to remember which one . . .'

While she paused there passed across her face something which some observer might have said was a hint of a smile. Brixton saw it and was grateful: he was trying to 'collect' himself: he had never supposed that Trig the old faggot might one day 'forget herself, embarrass him with her talk—hints about rude things.

'It's my turn to speak, Mr Brake,' she went on. 'And don't you be shy. I can speak to Mr Brake because he is one of my own kind. Don't be taken in by me as an ex-married woman, Mr Brake —I know, none better, all that side of life, I know what the woman meant in her matrimonial advertisement—she said she wanted to meet a man, one well-hung. Well, why not? The animals do it, and why shouldn't we? Horses are *very* well-hung, and if you have never seen a pair in action you should. But there you are, what a contradiction, my heart was never in it! They say you can't go against nature without paying a penalty—but what do you do about *two* natures? I mean when nature takes it into her head to send us off in two opposite directions? And don't pretend you don't understand, Mr Brake. A man well-hung! Don't tell me you wouldn't be interested!

There was again the hint, perhaps even the promise of a smile; but Brixton, uneasy in the other chair was informing himself that rude things were rude things—well, he was quite partial to a bit of smut, only he preferred it to be on the mild side when it came from a lady (only perhaps you could say about Trig that she could be better described as a woman who was no lady. Well, he didn't know. But well-hung! Well, blow a man down if the old he-bitch wasn't bang on! But never mind, over all the years of his life he had escaped being hen-pecked—and now if nobody minded he wasn't going to end up being bitch-worried!)

'I give you credit, Mr Brake. For not being a dumb-bell, as it used to be said in my day. There's a thousand nobody need ever talk to—that's without a miracle happening. And here I am talking to you, Mr Brake, and that's a compliment. And you can talk back Mr Brake, if it pleases you. But if you insist on caution and reserve I don't disagree. Oh yes, I would say there's a long long way to go in this country before we see men's liberation. I would never want to see you in trouble with the law, Mr Brake.'

But this last was too close to the knuckle and a good deal more than Brixton could take—well, there was this Rusling affair, and a funny business that, a man just didn't know. And the two demons had treated him pretty rough—well twisted his arm, see! Hinted! It wasn't the sort of thing they would expect him to be up to, but they didn't know (and by God the same old thing he always told himself!) Like taking dope, they said, beginning on grass, one thing could lead to another. Watch your step, Brake! Be very careful, watch it! And now damn it for the first time here was old Trigger turning out just another of life's menaces—instead of being the comfort he had come to expect (and thankful too). It was all too hard on his nerves—but when he began haltingly to excuse himself she leaned suddenly forward, taking his wrists in a grip more powerful than his own.

'Mr Brake, I apologize! It's my day, I told you it's my day to speak—and then I made my mistake, I spoke about you when I had decided upon my own day of self-indulgence. As for you, Mr Brake, a fig for policemen and the things people do and policemen try to find out about. Let them go and look at the horses if they are interested in genitals—it would do them good. But who wouldn't prefer to see (as if anyone could!) what another organ was up to?—and a more important one too if I may say so without sounding like something you might see on the grocer's calendar for the month of September. Springtime, Mr Brake. And I refer to the human heart. And not quite the same sort of organ we share with the animals—well, it's the difference that makes us human wouldn't you say, Mr Brake? Perhaps it *is* a bit late in the day, but I don't ever forget what my own has been up to in its time. And neither do you, Mr Brake, unless I am making a bad mistake. But not the sort of thing to be discussed with a policeman . . .'

And it was then, when it was as though her voice had failed her, that Brixton saw something he had never seen or expected to see, which had never been included in any memories or imaginings of the features of Mrs Trigger. He saw the tears which grew in size until they slid and jolted on the rugged texture of her cheeks. And never before short of words, it was now his strange difficulty that he could not induce his lips to move. But if Mrs Trigger suffered the same kind of difficulty it was very temporary.

'Mr Brake, I am a very guilty woman. Yes, guilty, because I see now that many years ago I seriously misjudged the strength and wearing quality of my heart's affections. So now I intend at this late hour in the day my penance—I will prove to myself and the world that I can make some amends. Give me time and I will leave nobody in any doubt that I know the identity of the one who has killed our dearest little Mrs Rusling. If you will allow me one minute to get my breath back Mr Brake, I will tell you . . .'

With her eyes closed and head thrown back it was as though she had been ' removed ' by the spell of her own rhetoric: she ' returned ' and opened her eyes, but there was no Brixton. It had all been too much for him and he had removed himself in the more usual sense, and very silently on his soft fancy shoes. Not even the promise of a dramatic revelation had been sufficient to detain him.

When all said and done he didn't know. There were mad people in the world—and a man had to watch out. Or else. And he reminded himself there was no saner pensioner inhabited the village . . .

Tups and his off-sider were fortunate enough to be much informed by the young orderly on duty at the morgue while they awaited the arrival of the doctor who had been phoned for. But of course, not a word! And in fact the young man, Greensworth by name, was not unknown to the two men, since he had not long ago had to pay quite a fine for throwing a bottle into a celebrating crowd on New Year's Eve. (But it seemed he had now decided upon a contrary line of behaviour, wishing only to remain in a steady job so long as it was socially useful: he was in no doubt that the hospital job fitted the requirement—well, there could be no question: and indeed you had only to look at the battery of doors behind which bodies were lying on sliding racks at the right temperature for preservation: a temporary state of course, but one which for a variety of reasons might be much prolonged.)

When the two demons entered the out-of-date public-lavatory kind of building, gloomy and damp and very chilly, one of the doors in the series was open, and there confronted them a pair of feet on a rack a little withdrawn from its cavern, with two big toes tied together so that feet might not fall apart. After prompt recognition, there were pleasantries while the young man, who had beautiful long hair that shone and curled, and was confined by a red knitted headband, told them details of his job, demonstrating by opening more doors behind which more big toes were fastened together: it also appeared to please him to show how smoothly the racks would slide in and out. And the policemen could not but approve of any young man doing such a useful job: their sparse comments were to be interpreted as compliments. But since the promised doctor was such an unconscionable time in turning up, it was unfortunate that young Greensworth and his affairs were soon again all in doubt. Because although there was no new affair of bottle-throwing, it appeared that he remained anti-establishment after all: he was interested in his work, true, and intended to remain and perform all duties required of him in a thoroughly workmanlike manner. But he felt it his duty to insist that it was only fair for other establishment workers equally to pull their weight: and in this particular example who should appear to fall down most on the job?—why none other than the public hospital medical staff!

Now in the view of the detectives (although more especially Tups—after all, along at the Film Society Ringer had seen many up-to-date screenings of subversive modern cinema), this was not quite the sort of young man's reformation they could approve of. Subversion was subversion wherever it might rear its ugly head.

But for all that the two men were sharp enough to see themselves in something of a dilemma—because Greensworth, bitter, he said, because qualified men did a damn sight poorer preserving job for human life than he did for human remains, was soon very free with information about reasons for the delay in a report upon the mysterious demise of Mrs Rusling.

'Well you know,' the young man, 'where large-scale organization is this size a lot of people never have a notion whether they are coming or going.'

But then he interrupted himself by indulging in a smile that temporarily abolished his very straight face. And it could have been his tit for tat—for the bull-dozer kind of questioning aimed at him at the time of his bottle-throwing. Maybe. But no matter, the two men's front of patience remained unfaulted.

'Yes,' Greensworth went on, 'the big-shot who keeps an eye on these jobs is away on holiday or something, so there's Scobie, younger man, his off-sider—clever they say, but he's got peculiar eyesight. Can't see a thing unless it's half a mile off. Well, there's this case of the lady-killer with the rubber knife-handle—and Scobie turns up with his wrong pair of specs. Too bad, he's left the right ones at home that day. But still, he goes ahead, the entire works and what a mess—you should see! But anyhow he can't find a thing wrong, not a one—or so I've been told. Well of course if you ask me, no seeing, no finding—simple as that. Not for me to say is it?—I mean what would a capitalist-industrialist-society cipher know about a thing like that! But do you know something? This Scobie character now turns out to be a very sick man—or so they say, and maybe he picked up a bug from one of his post-mortems (or should that word be mortes, don't ask me). I wouldn't know which one. But I wouldn't be surprised—they can be very messy, and I've seen the young quacks scared white. Just in case of picking up something pretty coc-eye.'

His pause was this time very long, and accompanied by his again abandoning his straight face. It could have pleased him that now the two men's front showed signs of cracking: it was clear that Tups especially was trying very hard to hold it.

Greensworth resumed his familiar face.

'Excuse me officer,' he said, 'but a man has to watch his step. I put a foot wrong and then what? I could be demoted to the receiving end of the chute where they toss in the dirty linen from infectious diseases, top floor. It is not my wish to remain in this institution as a case of cholera leprosy whathaveyou or worse—buboes the size of tennis balls under me armpits. But you know, you'd be surprised—who was it put the cat among the pigeons? Well, blowing my own trumpet's not my thing, but what with Scobie's eyesight what would have been the story if I hadn't kept my own peepers open? Because there it was all over, just another cadaver after due attention, the full works, and one leg a bit swollen you could see—although you couldn't blame the young quack seeing he'd forgotten to bring his glasses. Yes, but I could see—sticking plaster on the calf of that leg, although nothing much to notice I will admit, and the same about the colour of the leg if you ask the orderly. So I thought then, okay, *over* to the orderly and I peeled the plaster off, with me rubber gloves mind you, and put it away in me empty pay packet. And it all goes to show I've got a social conscience don't you reckon?—because I rang up this Scobie, told him the works, and where to find the packet by the telephone if he was interested. And next day it wasn't where I'd left it. Nobody's told me a thing—that's it so far as I'm concerned. But I'll tell you something—I've never heard another thing, but nota bene, I've never seen a bad scratch that looked like the one on the lady's leg. Well, not a big cut, but the muscle was all bunched up and trying to bulge out, I've never seen anything like it . . .'

And now, having told his story, the young man, after briefly indulging himself once more in a change from his straight face, became morose and complaining. The job was no catch: either there was too much to do or not enough: it was not like working on the industrial assembly-line, that was admitted: there was what you could call a constant supply of cadavers, but it was irregular: and he did not think a change could be expected from any attempt to introduce rationalization. Computers would probably be use-less—and in any case the trouble was most likely to be located in two words: assembly, dissembly. It was the dissembly-line he worked on: and perhaps after all he was wrong in his prejudices about the dirty linen that came down the chute from the infectious diseases ward—because if dissembly was the dialectical opposite of assembly, then it would be good logic for him to go and *ask* for the job at the receiving end of the chute—because action re-action, capitalism communism, assembly dissembly—you couldn't get away from the dialectic no matter how you tried. Everybody's turn came for dissembly, see—you mightn't go and ask for it but you could still bet on it. And who knew better than he did there was absolutely nothing to write home about on the assembly-line? So why not accept the existential logic, and end up on the dis-sembly-line once and for all . . .

But the two officers had had enough, and the more especially as Greensworth had reached beneath his apron for a grubby paper-back. The two men had been dismissed but they could be good-humoured about it—well, fair exchange, they had been much informed. But each was at pains to note the kind of book—and neither political nor sexual subversion, at least nothing serious, not really: an angry young poet with long hair, whose slender arms enclosed a naked child against his naked torso. Tups' nuance (which shaded indifference into distaste), was almost impossible to discern. It could be more readily concluded that Ringer was curious: he would remember the picture, perhaps the young poet's American-sounding name: after all he was with-it, a paid-up member of the Film Society . . .

And it was then the telephone rang, a message for Detective-Inspector Tupsall please. Would he contact the following day, when the information he wanted would be available? . . .

The word was no sooner around that Mrs Trigger had ceased to be invisible than it was clear too she was on the rampage. Not the thing to be expected, and indeed quite out of character: it was part of the Establishment of the village that at any given moment of the day there could never be any doubt what she was up to. Well, knitting—but it was easy to fill in the odd twenty minutes or half an hour when she was not on public view: there

could be a cup of tea, or she must cut herself a slice of bread—
and it went without saying she had no convenient husband to send
out with a string bag to do the shopping. (There was no husband
in the settlement nor for that matter any single man who used a
trundle, a convenience which appeared proper only for the other
sex. But it appeared that even a string bag could have its embarrass-
ments: there was a story that old Miss McCarroll, who it was
said would never see eighty again, had met in the supermarket
buying corn beef old Mr Stainley—a taciturn bachelor who shook
and stumbled and walked with a stick. And Miss McC's kind and
quavering offer had been overheard. Could Mr Stainley manage?
Would he like to put his meat into her trundle, and his full kit as
well if he cared to?)

But perhaps the word rampage was not altogether the right
one, because Mrs Trigger most easily and affably passed the time
of day with those she visited, and it was not until she asked about
Mr Hornley and his first-aid services, curious to know whether
they encouraged the man, or whether he offered and insisted,
that she became excited. And more than anything else, could they
remember about his bandages and dressings and what he used
for disinfectant? She hoped that nobody had been so foolish as
to pay him money.

In next to no-time there was nobody in the village she hadn't
visited—and that was to say nobody that Mr Hornley during his
many months of caring hadn't either (although there were the
exceptions that were to be taken for granted, Mr Piper Mr Brake
and Mr Hornley himself: nobody ever visited the first, and for
her own very private reasons Mrs Trigger would not be the first
to break the rule: as for Mr Brake she could ask him her questions
as it suited her convenience when he appeared at her window:
and Mr Hornley—ah! There would be time enough and to spare
for that gentleman! In the meantime let him wait!)

It was for all that noticed that when Mrs Trigger's quick round
of visits was over she did not resume her customary o.p. Not a
bit of it—and immediately the story was about: she was leaving
the village early each morning and sometimes not returning until
late afternoon: and this strange behaviour from somebody whose
brief absences had formerly been very limited! There was rumour
and counter-rumour, and again in no-time it was known that

Mrs Trigger was inquiring about the neighbourhood, trying to discover what inhabitants had been favoured with the first-aid attentions of Mr Hornley. There had been however an expedition much further abroad about which the village had heard no gossip at all, a prolonged visit to poor Clem's carrier—who it was distressing to discover remained a very sad and forlorn man after suffering his loss of the woman who had been solace and compensation for a miserable domestic life.

It can be truthfully said of Mrs Trigger that although she had been on the earth's surface for nearly seventy years, she had remained a stranger to the full reality of suffering until that day when the detective informed her of the former identity of the late Mrs Rusling. The great receding landscape of a long lifetime, about which in retrospective mood she might have little to say in favour (but then equally, nothing much to say against), had suddenly been rendered a barren and desolate waste, in awful truth a terrifying nightmare. And perhaps, worst of all, all because of her own fault! A long long time ago a young heart had been touched, she had been quickened with tenderness and devotion, with love, and . . . But pointless to remember now—now it was cool reason and impartial justice she was concerned with. Let her have all her wits about her! Let her instinct for what had to be justly done be acted upon in the clear cold light of reason! Yet now, confronted by that great desolate lump of humanity, what sort of a grip could she retain on her good resolutions? The pathos of the huge clumsy-appearing man was almost not to be believed —where now was the dignity of days when she had seen him deliver Clem her daily parcel? Alas! As Mr Brake would say he had folded. Although perhaps not folded (how could any such lump fold?) No, it was inward collapse, what the new scientists called an implosion, the bone structure had broken down and been absorbed into all that vast jelly of flesh (and despite his girth he had stood up straight and proud, as though confident about the strength dignity and efficacy of his own labour). He reminded Mrs Trigger (some part of her searching anxiously for relief, and comic for preference), of somebody long long ago, somebody who stood out clearly even though far away back on her lifetime landscape—and indeed a comic figure of the old moving picture days: somebody about the same size, and on his

78

face the same troubled look of near-imbecile simplicity: it almost made her laugh out loud to remember the tip of his right index finger in his mouth! It was Fatty Arbuckle—and it astonished her that all was as though consciously tried for!

Were there questions to be answered about the first-aid services of Mr Hornley?—then go ahead, ask away. Although mind you, there was nothing much to remember: Pet, that was Mrs R, had scratched her leg on the rough edge of her kitchen tidy. Hornley— and you know (and it said something for the distressed man that he removed his finger from his mouth and smiled)—well, you know, give him the liberty, Hornley, and you wouldn't would you expect to see him with anything against running a hand round a lady's leg. Well, where's the harm? You know the old gag— why does a woman sometimes wear her wrist watch on her ankle? Well, it's because of the hands.

Mrs Trigger exclaimed. She was no prude! No, but it was offensive that this levity should accompany convincing appearances of hopeless grief.

There was in any case little to tell, only that Pet had allowed Hornley to bandage until the fatal day—when she had decided healing might be hastened if the sore was left exposed to the air for a change, although with a plaster patch on at night so as not to soil the sheets. And he remembered, yes, she had a bad pain all down the leg, it was like sciatica she had said, only worse, and there was swelling . . .

And it had to be left at that because of a caller, a young nurse on social service duty, who in the very briefest of mini-skirts stepped out of her smart and shining mini-car: she was cool collected and shapely, with clear eyes, and smooth hair done into a bun in a net. She had with her a plastic bag that contained a large plastic overall, and it was her mission to bath the wrecked and termagant wife. And after Mrs Trigger had introduced her-self as one with nursing experience her kind offer to assist was accepted, an office usually performed by the large husband—and now indeed once again performed by him, for the unfortunate woman immediately challenged fight, and screamed and bit with such vigour that Mrs Trigger was obliged to retreat: whereupon John Whiteman at the same time as he assisted soothed with such gentleness of language and action that Mrs Trigger was moved, and had to cover up by taking a broom and vigorously banging about as she swept out the kitchen, the place where they had sat while they talked. But despite the generous well-wishings of her rough manly heart, Mrs Trigger was busy in her head with a string of condemnations. She was shocked by and she deplored the filthy condition of the house: that great strong man had gone all to pieces—with his means of livelihood seriously threatened: his great broken-down-looking van in the backyard was as though beleagured by piles of assorted rubbish, vegetable and mineral, a kind of distorted mirror-image to the inside disorder of his kitchen, where the piled-up unwashed dishes and cooking things were all the nastier for having been there for days . . .

And when it was all over, and Mrs Trigger was saying her goodbyes in the dreadful backyard, who should appear but the son of the house! Lithe and tall, sharpfeatured, with sunk cheeks blank eyes and long hair all in rat-tails, and all these features the same non-colour, he said he was glad to see the lady on the way out: he had no time for oldie females and not when they went in for whoring either—which should be prohibited when they were as old as the age when they ought to be dead . . .

And Mrs Trigger behaved marvellously, never better in her life: without answering back, with grace and dignity she silently and most solemnly bowed to the young man.

But all the way home to the village thoughts fixed themselves upon three vivid images. There was John Whiteman, a man she could by no means bring herself to dislike despite every prejudice —for there was some kind of subterraneous relation to her Trigger, whom she would always remember as a man (at any rate the *kind* of man), who could be tolerated: the second was Pet Rusling (and it was curious that it was *Pet* Rusling—just like that, not *Clem*, and definitely not Jess Barrow). Anyhow a person she could not bring herself to dislike either—for after all, bygones had to be bygones or life would become quite intolerable (and one could do nothing better than go and take an overdose): this bygone had well and truly gone, there was no more an image in her mind of the little powder-puff, and so long ago: instead, clearly, somebody Rusling, aging, shapeless, grey-blonde, charming: she could no longer keenly lament and suffer that death had intervened, no—because what had this elderly person to do with the third image in her mind, and the dominant one, a vigorous handsome young woman, one Amy Piper, horse-riding, healthy, a qualified nurse with many many years of interesting life to come . . .

It was misfortune for Brixton that he should land himself in a sticky situation while there was still the infuriating Hospital-delay with the post-mortem report. Detective-Inspector Tupsall had not for years been in such an unhealthy state of controlled (but only just), fury. From all directions there were always the pressures of his job—well, true, and that was what in more than thirty years he had become accustomed to: but what he now found most of all intolerable in these late days of his career was the new kind of young press-reporter: brazen young people, and it was not always clear what sex: at first he had supposed a few harmless humorous digs about funny hair and fancy clothes would not be amiss, take some of the bounce out of the young hounds, wipe the grins off their faces, but not a bit of it!—they never turned a long hair, remained cocky confident and not too faintly contemptuous. And perhaps worst of all was that they had no proper education; and even worse still when they sometimes claimed to have a university degree: there were times when they had to ask what the words that came natural to you meant, even how to spell. And then when you asked to see what they had written down—my God!

No! And again, No!

It was however not quite so bad for Ringer, not such a generation gap. And sometimes too Ringer was minded to take liberties with his senior which, pushed only a shade further, could have landed him on the mat. When Ringer put on an act in which he figured faintly on the side of the younger media-men (even perhaps in slight favour of the young hound up for indecency rape drugs blackmail robbery violence breaking-in), then according to the severity of the pressures and strains of the moment it could have been a thing which required only one more twist, one extra bit of pressure, and Tups would have been right around the bend.

So it was not one bit good for Brixton that late one night a young constable had dragged him in. It was not good, it was worse, indeed quite bad—Brixton had been spotted while engaged

upon a private occasion in the makeshift privacy of the Town
Belt's ill-lit leafy centre. Alas, if only the young policeman had
not been so keen to please his superiors and advance his career!
He had, he said, seen with his own eyes (but it was too bad that
the arrested man's partner in pleasure had been a little too quick,
managing to elude capture either by temporarily hiding in or
escaping through the Belt's dense greenery).

So what was the evidence?

Well, what the policeman could swear to have seen: what
Brixton had been persuaded to say in a statement (but which he
had afterwards very annoyingly refused to put his name to): and
what had been discovered when he had been formally arrested—
that he still had two buttons undone.

After a restless night of scratching while wrapped in a deplor-
ably-smelling off-colour blanket, and very bleary from no sleep, he
was next morning turned out into the open yard along with others
brought in overnight: and Tupsall and Ringer were among the
bunch of demons looking them all over just in case there might
be somebody they were wanting. And the Brake man was no
surprise (although there was a sense in which he was, and indeed
it was some moments before he was recognized: for Brixton was
as it were in 'transformation,' and that was to say his cap and
his binoculars were hidden in the Belt's greenery, and the sheen
of his leather jacket in reverse made him appear not quite of this
world in the context of the bare cement yard and dull morning
light: and the great fuzz of his hair was another thing not immediately to be believed in). But in a moment or two all was con-
versational, Ringer mock-sorry and smiling a little. After all,
hadn't he had his warning? Tups did not smile. Here was another
of them—and caught out. Ah well, it wasn't going to help in the
Rusling affair—but never mind, the law must take its course
(and the thought of Tups readily threw off many such original
thoughts): there were plenty of people in the community to catch
up with, bad lots, law-breakers—why, what if any ordinary sort
of man was to let himself go, go away and do the sort of thing
that might come into any man's head? It wouldn't do: nor do any
harm if that pervert was put away for a spell, it might even teach
him a lesson: although the man (if you could call him that),
might be lucky enough to get off with a fine—these days, it just

showed you! But perhaps a stiffish fine, and if he couldn't find the cash he could go to gaol anyhow . . . But Ringer's thoughts if they had been visible could have shown a colour of liberalism: after all, if they liked to please themselves on the quiet . . . And it came into his mind—once when he was drunk, an afternoon of celebration in a private bar. Six junior detectives, and one of them was being transferred, so an afternoon of farewell and no expense spared. Hard liquor! And young Rory, the one they would be parting with, had made them all laugh! Well, one time at the pictures, he had said—he had had to push along a whole row of people to the one empty seat right against the wall. Excuse please, excuse me madam, excuse me sir . . . and dammit, he had hardly time to settle down (and that was a picture! *Ryan's Daughter*, sexy as they come), and then hello hello hello, pressure from the leg next door, in next to no time there was a hand. Anyhow full house, rape on the screen, or it could have been mutual, just plain rooting. Anyway very tense, a pin could have been heard. Well, did he make an arrest? Call for lights up? Not on your nelly, no! Well, what would *you* have done? Go on, tell me! And after a silence somebody said, What *did* you do, Rory? And the chuckles began. Do! What do you mean *do*? Well, what could I do? And in reply to his grin catcalls, hoots of laughing. Whoopee!

But it turned out that Brixton was not to be so readily disposed of. He recovered from his shock and there came the usual comforting reassurance—he wasn't ignorant! Now was the time for all those Library books to come in handy: there was too his long habit of attending lectures, and he had lately at one of these listened to and greatly admired a liberal lawyer who had spoken fluently and with great emphasis about varieties of human behaviour, and the urgent need for society to tolerate its minorities—and more, appreciate their worth (among these groups were to be found many individuals of singular gifts). Brixton had been quick to get the message, and it had especially interested him that the speaker had said the future of the world and mankind was these days menaced by the big multiplying majority—and a good deal more than by the comparative few whose deviant behaviour did not contribute to over-population, increasing pollution, and the constant catching-up drives for more development, all adding up to the more and more serious exploitation and depletion of the

world's natural resources. After his library-lifetime, Brixton could
translate this kind of talk into another lingo—his own, which was
now spot-on concerning his chances of getting out of the nasty
jam in which he found himself. He was by no means broke (for
the most part thanks to kind and grateful benefactions from a
small assortment of Mr Woollies)—also for a few days he was
at large upon his own recognisance, although subject to daily
reporting to the police. And when he tried, it turned out surprisingly easy to see the liberal lawyer, who readily agreed to
assist him: at the same time saying that his chances might improve
before a jury compared to what a magistrate might decide. Fortunately too an upper court session was soon to begin, so he would
not have long to wait before his case was decided one way or the
other.

But despite the very few days he must wait according to the
calendar, Brixton now suffered a monotonous and sterile drag of
time; and never having been previously singled out by the law,
he experienced a loneliness more desolating than anything he
could remember. It was all very well to visit the Library and consult books where there was comfort and encouragement for anyone
who might be at risk (and among much else, Brixton had discovered the Danny Deever-like piece of poetry about the man who
had been put in gaol for having hair of the wrong colour)— it was
all very well, but it was all on paper, a very different and not at
present very hopeful thing, not when he would soon have to take
his own chance in court. In the meantime he must report every
day to the police and who knew?—once there was publicity, and
perhaps even though the verdict turned out to be not guilty, he
might find himself the sort of person nobody would want to see
living in a pensioner settlement.

And in his distress the at first astonishing thought occurred to
him—that he would not be doing himself any additional harm
if he talked to old Trig: after all there was a something, perhaps
a nothing, you mightn't be able to put your finger on it, but . . .

When after many hesitations Brixton began to talk to Trig,
circumlocuting, she pulled at the parchment of her cheeks, twisted
her withered lips, and so much looked the savage that he was
reminded of some old Maori chief of either sex painted by
Lindauer: he was interrupting, she said: she was sitting for just

84

a few short moments while she collected her thoughts, then she must be up and away. What *was* Mr Brake trying to say? But to remove for a second or two her attention from the stitches she was casting off and look into the man's face was to be moved. There was something wrong: there was stamped on the man's face a shadow, something not to be defined, yet something there even though not even surely perceived. And there was her sudden understanding—the man was in great trouble, he (and in these latter days the word came more readily to mind), suffered. He needed help, and he would get it—only first let him cease to mumble as though trying to make what he had to say unintelligible. Mumble mumble. What there was of colour in his face had disappeared, and he was talking in some kind of wound-up puppet language (the sort of thing that that Algy over there might speak if he could) which would never cease to go on and on. Mumble mumble mumble. But she knew it was not like Algy— the man was talking of his misery.

And very soon Mrs Trigger knew. Not so very long ago she had spoken her own piece and now Brixton was speaking his, and while he mumbled she did not interrupt. Until very lately, through all her years, she had preferred to know little about the concealed depths of misery in her own heart: now she was suffering as much from the revelation of ignorance as the pain which had been the revealing agent: and now too it seemed that she had no sooner been forced into silent admission by that terrible policeman, than she had recognized in the great clumsy carrier miseries which she would never dare to say were less severe than her own: and as though all that was not enough here she was all over again encountering the very same thing.

In Mrs Trigger's book of rules there was a contradiction which said that the remedy for almost any kind of irredeemably sticky situation was prompt action. Clearly it was not necessary for Brixton to say one word more. Knowing now quite accurately what his trouble was all about (and since there was a policeman at the bottom of it there could be no question which side she was on), Mrs Trigger announced to herself her intention of doing what she could to help. Money? A good lawyer? And certainly when the time came she would afford him the support of her personal presence in court, that was to say if he had no objections. But in the meantime! And speaking now her own surprising confidences, she explained there was another injustice to be remedied—she had not yet caught up with the slayer of that poor darling Mrs Rusling, done to death by . . . But discretion prompted that it was not yet time, not yet awhile—she must guard her tongue and make no direct mention of names. Anyhow, there it was, a fine day, neither too hot nor too cold, another good day for her unfinished task of doing the streets first on one side and then the other, and all to discover where the Hornley man had been with his first-aid. And now with Mr Brake's kind help her task would be cut in half . . .

And surely such marvellous good fortune could never have been anticipated!—it was Brixton who knocked on the door behind which information of momentous importance awaited them. Why yes (the young housewife's tottering baby could not reach mother's mini-skirt, so instead sat down and cried), yes, Mr Hornley, that was the name. And when Mrs Trigger had been summoned from across the street information was supplied. Mr Hornley, a smiling little man and *very* obliging. He used to come from the Village and bring his bandages and disinfectants—besides lollies and apples for the children, yes. And everything very neat in a little home-made wooden box with a handle. And oh dear, poor grandpa!—for all his years so devoted to his garden. But one day wearing sand shoes he should not have been wearing because they were worn out he had cut his poor foot on something sharp and rusty—and even worse as it turned out, for it had been inside a bag of farmyard manure. Mr Hornley couldn't have been kinder, regular visits and he inspired confidence, real professional, and never leaving a mess because he always cleared up afterwards— he would take the swabs and bandages to burn them, so he said. And so *many* bandages, such an expense! And he would never accept any money.

And Mrs Trigger was holding a large breath. She had several times encountered much the same story, and now refused to believe in any good fortune until it was well and truly within her grasp.

After all, Mr Hornley's *other* patients seemed all to have evaded their allotted doom, they had all safely recovered.

'And how is grandpa now?' she inquired.

The young woman hesitated, feeling for her handkerchief.

'Oh dear,' he said. 'He died, yes. He's dead. The doctor rushed

him into hospital, but he died. It was sad—something very unusual, they said. Gas gangrene, that's what they said it was. Yes,
fatal.'

Having had to change buses twice instead of just the once (as
she had been misinformed), Mrs Trigger did not arrive in court
until Brixton's case was about to be called. Also, there had been
additional delay, for, finding herself right in the city it had
occurred to her to call at the central police station. There was her
medicine chest to demand back; but then too, since the newspapers
had for some days ceased to report any more the strange delay
in establishing cause of death in the Rusling affair, she was
beginning to suspect those two policemen were hoping their in-
competence would remain unexposed while public interest was
switched to other matters : perhaps some fire or flood, or six people
including a three month baby all burned up in a road smash, or
more bombs whether over the tropics or in poor Belfast (where
grandparents on her mother's side had long ago emigrated
from). It was with pleasure that she anticipated asking to see
Mr Detective-Inspector Tupsall (or she would pretend to make a
mistake and say Topsail). Anyway it would be bang-on, because
let that gentleman just wait—and he would see the wind taken
right out of his canvas! Taking her medicine chest indeed!—
putting her under suspicion of administering a poisonous dose.
But what she would ask, and seeming very casual, was whether
or not there was any fresh news?—because it might interest them
to know that if *she* had been in charge of the case (although it was
none of her business of course), it wouldn't have been the *last*
thing she would have thought of doing—well, checking up on
that first aid kit of Mr Hornley's, *him*! carting around his plasters
and bandages, and taking them off to take home and burn, oh to be
sure, so he said, but more likely getting them all mixed up, clean
and dirty, forgetting which were used ones and which not. Infection! That was what *she* learned about when she was training
for a nurse. Infection! Nowadays it was all go ahead, hope for the
best, if in doubt give an anti-biotic, or rub it on, or there could
be the let-out of that sacred name, Virus!

But the two detectives were nowhere to be found at the station.
It had at first been Mrs Trigger's intention to accompany Brixton

from the moment he left the settlement that morning until he surrendered his bail at the court. But he had much resisted her proposal, insisting that he would be very glad if she came along and lent him her moral support, yes; but in the meantime, before his ordeal began, he would prefer an hour of solitude to think once again about his line of defence. But the awkward nub of the matter, about which he was silent, was his uncertainty and lack of resolution whenever his thoughts turned to the difficult question of his 'transformation.' It has already been mentioned that he had been arrested while transformed, and had retained that appearance until he had been before the magistrate : but once his bail had been arranged he had immediately gone and recovered his cap and binoculars from their hiding place underneath the Belt's greenery. Commonsense now assured him that he would not be permitted to appear before judge and jury wearing these items : but there was another sense (and perhaps one not so common), which prompted him to decide that he must have them ready and close at hand in case of some direful emergency, the nature of which he could not foresee, but which might well be suddenly upon him without warning. And so it was that there he was, punctually on time and surrendering to the constable court-orderly with the showy mother-of-pearl side of his jacket on view, and the honorary Polynesian side of his character further established with his fuzz of hair (although there were street acquaintances who assured him that his hair-do was a good deal more professionally Afro than Polynesian): it was an appearance which he was secretly proud of, and the more particularly because it was associated with modest earnings so very necessary to supplement his pension. But for all that, inside his jacket and held under one armpit there was his leather cap; and suspended a little below the other (believe it or not), were his binoculars.

When Mrs Trigger at last arrived at the court (many old buildings had been lately demolished and many old streets much altered, and she had inquired and misunderstood many directions), she could at first make nothing of what went on. There was noise and confusion, many citizens called for jury-service standing around and introducing themselves one to the other—complaining about a waste of time, and the pay was poor although better than it had been. There were also policemen, besides lawyers in their wigs and gowns, chatting in groups among tables and chairs. There was nobody sitting, and Mrs Trigger (the only representative of her sex except for three prospective jurywomen), much in need of resting her legs, might well have been the first to find somewhere to sit if it hadn't been that now there was a new kind of commotion, with a corroding male voice ordering silence. Voices were stilled, and there was a shuffle of feet as all the company turned in the same direction and stood to attention. It was the wigged and gowned judge who entered; and who, before seating himself at his elevated bench bowed to everyone, and was himself by everyone bowed to. By everyone except Mrs Trigger that is to say, for her attention was focused totally upon Brixton who, elevated a good head and shoulders above all the standing company had suddenly become visible in the large raised enclosure known as the dock. And although some extra sense informed Mrs Trigger that this male person *was* Brixton, she was nonetheless informing herself he was no Brixton she had previously set eyes upon. And the puzzle of this transformed person, so much focused yet at the same time confused her attention, that she was oblivious first to the voice of the registrar of the court as he read out the charge and asked the prisoner to plead : and then to the new confusing matter which was the calling of names of prospective jurymen who would function unless challenged either by the prosecution or the prisoner. And now it happened that perhaps at first there was nobody in the court to notice (nobody that is to say except Mrs Trigger)—to notice that instead of continuing to stand statue-still Brixton was suddenly confining his honorary Polynesian hair beneath his familiar cap, besides very rapidly reversing his jacket—and then hey presto! his binoculars were as usual slung from his neck. And how could he be aware of the corroding male voice that demanded he immediately take off his hat!—how could he when so much occupied doing the only thing to come into his mind that he could do? He was trying to be nice to Mr Woolly. There was in Brixton, and there always had been, something profoundly well-wishing and kindly, very considerate : he had never in all his life given the name of love to any emotion he had felt; after all, he was that sort of Kiwi, who has the most embarrassing difficulty with the word, and on that account inclines to settle for something reduced—so that, although the emotion

89

remains the same, the diminished word renders it more manageable. Mr Woolly had many times been very kind to him (and that word, kind, it was the better, the more manageable word)—and he too after his own fashion had been kind to Mr Woolly. And now it had most surprisingly turned out that he was not himself so much in trouble, no, it was Mr Woolly—and without any doubt he must do all in his power to help. And so if he quickly became another person, one quite unknown to Mr Woolly, that could be a very good and kindly way of helping. Why, he had been confided in, helped with money; he had enclosed this old man in his arms, soothing, lending a considerate hand to dry away tears (after a troubled account of matrimonial and family difficulties)—until, the crisis over and something like equilibrium restored, they could devote the hours to consoling conversation about this and that, things that concerned them. There was something to a man's life after all, he could be useful, the barriers could sometimes come down, all that was too solitary with nobody caring could be temporarily defeated and sent packing . . .

But meanwhile many had noticed: the judge was very still, an elbow on the bench, and his head leaning a little sideways against his propping arm and hand. And his eyes were staring— it seemed in the direction of the prisoner. A court-orderly constable spoke to the registrar, and the registrar stood up and turned and spoke to the judge, who did not reply. And then the registrar reached to touch the judge's arm, and so interfered with the prop to his head.

A horrid clatter was accompanied by a sudden collective gasp, and then for one brief moment all was dramatically silent. Like a showman's puppet the judge had disappeared from view—disappeared into whatever depths might be concealed behind his judicial bench.

Mrs Trigger waited and waited—and waited until the court except for herself was empty. So much had gone on, such a buzz of conversation, with the corroding male voice not insisting upon silence until another judge had been found. He said briefly he was adjourning the court, excusing the jury in the meantime. And Brixton had been popped in and out of the dock, up and down a stairway several times over—until at last he was down and it seemed out of sight for ever. But his lawyer now appeared, approaching Mrs Trigger, saying that he had a message—Mr Brake would be glad if she would wait, an extension of bail was being arranged, it wouldn't be long now . . .

And soon he joined her, pulling on his cap, reversing his jacket, arranging his binoculars, wanting to know if she had any news about Mr Woolly—but beg pardon, he meant the judge.

Mrs Trigger knew nothing except gossip. There had been talk of a fatal stroke: others said the judge had fainted: there was an old man who remembered when he was a boy back in Ireland, he had seen somebody affected exactly the same way as the judge —and it was an old witch of a woman who had fixed him with her Evil Eye . . . But anyhow, there had been an ambulance.

Brixton mentioned he was feeling peckish, and he reckoned Mrs Trigger must be feeling much the same way, besides in need of a cuppa. So they joined in the extravagance of a taxi, and indulged themselves in two extras—first asking the man to wait while *they* waited for fish and chips; and then stopping again to buy four bottles of beer . . .

That evening there was much talk in the village: it was known by everyone that after a very unaccustomed arrival home the pair had spent the afternoon together in Mrs Trigger's flat: there had been the sound of much laughter, and bottles of beer had been seen on the window ledge.